GETTING EVEN WITH DAD

A NOVELIZATION BY JORDAN HOROWITZ
BASED ON THE SCREENPLAY WRITTEN BY
TOM S. PARKER & JIM JENNEWEIN

SCHOLASTIC INC.
New York Toronto London Auckland Sydney

MACAULAY CULKIN   TED DANSON

GETTING EVEN WITH DAD

METRO-GOLDWYN-MAYER Presents a JACOBS/GARDNER Production a HOWARD DEUTCH Film
MACAULAY CULKIN TED DANSON "GETTING EVEN WITH DAD"
GLENNE HEADLY SAUL RUBINEK GAILARD SARTAIN and HECTOR ELIZONDO Editor RICHARD HALSEY Production Designer VIRGINIA L. RANDOLPH Director of Photography TIM SUHRSTEDT
Executive Producer RICHARD HASHIMOTO Written by TOM S. PARKER & JIM JENNEWEIN Produced by KATIE JACOBS and PIERCE GARDNER Directed by HOWARD DEUTCH

ISBN 0-590-48262-9

12 11 10 9 8 7 6 5 4 3   4 5 6 7 8 9/9

Printed in the U.S.A.   40

First Scholastic printing, July 1994

Contents

1.
The Plotters

That morning, Ray Gleason took his usual midday break from his job at Wankmueller's Bakery. But instead of buying his usual lunch at the corner deli, he dusted the flour from his clothes and drove to a corner in downtown San Francisco.

His two friends, Carl and Bobbie, were waiting for him when he arrived. Across the street was a small office building. A construction chute from the second floor emptied down to a huge Dumpster in the alley. Ray, Carl, and Bobbie watched as some construction workers sent some old wallboard material down the chute.

"This crazy old lady lived alone down in Fremont," explained Ray as he and his two friends watched the building. "No friends, no relatives. Day the county buries her, nobody even shows. A couple days later someone from the state tax office comes poking around and sees this trunk in her attic. What's he find? A mother lode of rare coins. Totally uncirculated. Like they just came

1

out of the mint. Maybe her husband, who died a while back, had the coins from years ago. Maybe she didn't even know they were there.

"So being there's no relatives or will, the state confiscates 'em, right? And they're gonna sell 'em, auction 'em off. But before they do that, these coins have to be appraised. And that happens right here in San Francisco, at the Professional Coin Grading Service."

Ray was now pointing to the top of the small office building. "They're on the top floor," he told his friends. "Pickup's by armored car from the parking level, between five and six in the afternoon."

Bobbie, who was nervously bouncing from leg to leg, turned to Carl. "Hey, fashion plate," he said. "You got that?"

But Carl, a big man who always dressed in a suit and tie, and who had just wolfed down yet another sauerkraut-smothered hot dog, wasn't listening. Instead, he was blotting his tie with his handkerchief, trying to remove a bit of mustard. "Trick is to blot," explained Carl. "*Never* rub. This is silk. Cost me forty-five bucks."

Ray reached over and straightened Carl's tie. "Look, Carl," he said patiently. "We pull this off and you can buy a thousand silk ties. You can be the Silk Tie King from San Francisco Bay. But first you gotta pay some kind of attention here."

Carl folded his handkerchief neatly and put it away in his breast pocket. Ray was right. This was a big score they were planning, the biggest they had ever planned.

"I hear ya, Ray," said Carl. "I'm with the program."

That evening the three men met again at Ray's small apartment. Carl bought a pizza and immediately began shoving slices into his mouth. Bobbie paced back and forth, nervously smoking cigarettes. Ray was holding a newspaper called *The Numismatist Weekly*. All the articles were about coins and coin collecting. Its headline read COIN HORDE FOUND IN TRUNK, which Ray had circled in red ink.

"The question is," began Ray, "how much was this poor old widow worth when they buried her? The answer is a million five."

Carl stopped chewing. Bobbie exhaled a long wisp of smoke. That was more money than they had ever even imagined.

"That's seven hundred and fifty grand to us," explained Ray. "A quarter million apiece."

"Who's the fence?" asked Bobbie. He knew that half of the money would go to a special middle man who would take the coins and sell them for cash.

"A guy named Dobbs," answered Ray. "A specialist. Breaks the coins out of their holders so they can't be traced and moves 'em to dealers in Hong Kong and Europe."

Just then the phone rang. Carl reached over to answer it.

"Don't get that," said Ray. "It's probably Nadine."

"I thought you liked Nadine," said Carl.

"I did till she brought me that plant," replied Ray pointing to a sickly, yellowing elephant fern that sat on a table in a dark corner of the room. "See, when a woman gives you a plant, it's their little way of testing you. Like, if you can take care of it, it's a sign she can move the relationship to the next level. Believe me, when a woman gives you something you gotta water, feed, or take for a walk, it's time to dump her."

Carl looked at the plant. "It looks sick," he said.

"If it dies, it dies," shrugged Ray.

"Glad she didn't give you no cocker spaniel," said Carl. Then he scooped up another slice of pizza and aimed it into his mouth.

The next day Bobbie and Carl met Ray at the bakery. Ray's boss, Mr. Wankmueller, had gone to lunch, so the three men were able to talk freely.

"The coin auction is next Wednesday," said Ray as he squeezed frosting along a huge, three-tier wedding cake. "They're moving 'em from the

4

grading service to the auction house on Monday."

"So we grab the stuff while they're moving it," Bobby said. He was envisioning the excitement of stealing all those coins. "We hit an armored car. We'll need major firepower, a couple of AK-47's — "

"Bob," groaned Ray. "We're not invading Iraq. I'd like to do this job without wearing a flak jacket. Besides, we'd never find one Carl's size."

Bobbie frowned. He was looking forward to shooting guns and blowing up things. Meanwhile, Carl was scooping a glob of frosting from the wedding cake with his finger.

"Carl, don't poke the cake!" said Ray. "You know how long it took me to do this?"

Carl licked his finger. "You know, Ray," he said. "You're like that Michael dude, who did that ceiling."

"That Michael dude?" asked Ray. "Michelangelo? The Sistine Chapel?"

"But you paint with frosting," said Carl, nodding. He stared hungrily at the cake. "And that's *much* better."

Ray looked at the cake. In a way, he thought, Carl was right. He was a kind of artist. He was good at baking and decorating cakes. It was one of the good things he learned while he was in jail a few years earlier. When he got out, Mr. Wankmueller took a chance on him and gave him a job. Now he had the skills he needed to buy his own bakery and go straight for good.

But he needed money to buy his own shop. Lots of money. And to get it he knew he had to pull one more robbery. A big one.

The biggest one ever.

2.
Abducted by Aliens

Timmy Gleason, eleven years old, sat in the backseat of the '83 Cadillac, sipped his Pepsi, and looked out at the U.S. 5 highway. In the front seat, passenger side, was his aunt Kitty. She was nibbling on some french fries that were left over from the last rest stop. Next to her was Wayne, her new husband. Wayne had one hand on the steering wheel and the other around a double cheeseburger.

They were on their honeymoon and Timmy was wondering why they had to drag him along.

Bored out of his mind, Timmy picked up his camcorder and aimed it at the highway.

"Submitted for your approval," Timmy began narrating as if he were hosting *The Twilight Zone*. "Sunday, six P.M., a lonely stretch of California highway. Timmy Gleason suddenly realizes he'd been abducted by alien beings."

He leaned over the seat and aimed the camera at Wayne.

"The driver says his name is 'Wayne,'" he continued. "But Timmy knows he's really a hideous blob from another galaxy."

Wayne turned angrily to Timmy. "For the last time, get that thing out of my face!" he shouted. In the camera Wayne's mouth looked like a huge pit filled with half-chewed hamburger. "Sit back and be quiet!"

"Timmy, honey," begged Kitty. "Do what Wayne says."

Timmy frowned and sullenly sunk back into the seat. But he kept the camcorder running and aimed it upward from his lap.

"Sure Wayne *looked* human," he continued under his breath. "Right down to his bald spot. But Timmy knew it was all a disguise. No human could *ever* eat three double cheeseburgers in one sitting."

But Wayne had heard every word. "That does it!" he shouted. The veins in his temple looked about to burst. "Gimme that camera!"

Wayne reached back and tried to take the camera from Timmy with his free, though still greasy, hand. Timmy pulled the camera away. Suddenly Wayne lost control of the steering wheel and the Cadillac swerved. Timmy's soda went flying across the backseat.

Wayne managed to bring the car to a screeching stop along the side of the road. Then he turned and lunged at Timmy.

"Gimme that camera, you little jerk!" he ordered.

But Timmy kept the camera focused on Wayne with the power button turned on. "The alien lashes out," he narrated playfully. "He spewed secret sauce."

Just then the other alien appeared in Timmy's viewfinder. "Shut that camera off!" ordered his aunt.

Timmy obeyed. This alien meant business.

"He spilled soda all over the seat!" groaned Wayne.

"We'll clean it up, sweetheart," said Kitty, trying to calm her husband down. "There's a gas station up ahead. C'mon, honey."

Wayne stared at Timmy, but Timmy stared back defiantly. He didn't like this new husband of his aunt Kitty's and he wasn't keeping it a secret.

After pulling the car into the nearby gas station, Kitty told Timmy to go into the men's room and get all the paper towels he could find. Timmy climbed out of the car.

"I told you we shouldn't have brought him," he heard Wayne say as he walked toward the men's room.

"Nobody would take him," he heard his aunt reply. "What was I supposed to do with him?"

"I know what I'd like to do with him," Timmy

could still hear Wayne say. "I'd like to drive off and leave him here."

Timmy stopped when he heard those words. Now he knew that he didn't just dislike Wayne.

He *hated* him.

3.
The Surprise Guest

"All right, let me explain this one more time," said Ray as he spread the robbery plans out on his living room table. Bobbie and Carl studied the plans.

"Remember in high school science class the teacher did that little demonstration with rats in a maze?"

Carl looked at Ray with his blank expression. He had never gone to high school.

"Look," Ray continued. "All we're doing is creating a situation where we make the guards go exactly where we want 'em to go. Like — "

" — rats in a maze!" Carl blurted out. He understood now and was smiling.

"Right, right!" said Ray. He tapped a spot on the map. "They end up *here*. We do the grab. Nobody gets hurt, nothing goes wrong."

"That's what you said when we boosted those VCRs," Bobbie reminded Ray. "I do four years in Folsom Prison for stealing Betamaxes! It

11

wouldn't have been half bad if we got caught with VHS machines. You know, something we could *sell*. I mean, even the *judge* laughed at us."

"It was a mistake, okay?" said Ray, red-faced. "And you weren't the only one doing time. Remember that."

Bobbie and Carl exchanged glances. It was true that all three of them had gone to jail for that last job. Everyone had paid the price.

"Your guy Dobbs," began Bobbie. "What if he burns us?"

"He's not gonna burn us," replied Ray. "He's the one who turned me on to the job. I'm telling you, I got this wired. We walk in, we walk out. Nothing can possibly go wrong."

Just then there was a loud knock on the door. "Ray! Open up!" came a voice from the hallway. "It's Kitty! Your sister!"

Ray quickly rolled up the robbery plans and told Bobbie to hide them. Bobbie scurried about the room looking for a good hiding place. He finally stuffed the plans behind the couch cushions.

Ray opened the door. Kitty was standing there and she looked as if she was in a hurry.

"Kitty!" said Ray with surprise. He hadn't seen his sister in years. "How you doing? You look great!"

He reached over to hug her, but Kitty ignored him and rushed past him into the apartment.

"Skip the hugs and kisses, Ray," she said flatly.

"I don't got much time." Then she noticed Carl and Bobbie. "Who's Rocky and Bullwinkle?"

"Bobbie and Carl," began Ray. "My sister Kitty."

Carl waved a shy hello at Kitty. Bobbie blew a puff of smoke at her.

"So what're you doing in town?" asked Ray. "You should've called, told me you were coming."

"I *did* call," said Kitty. "About ten times, but you never answer your phone."

"He thought it was Nadine," said Carl. "She gave him a plant. Now Ray's all put out 'cause he hates the *big* commitment of watering it once a week."

"I got married, Ray," Kitty announced.

"No *kidding*," replied Ray. "That's great! When?"

"Three hours ago," answered his sister. "And I'm going on my honeymoon."

"Hi, Dad," came a tiny voice. All eyes turned toward the doorway. Timmy was standing there, holding a little suitcase, a backpack slung around his shoulder.

"*Dad??*" said Bobbie, stunned. He never even knew that Ray had a son.

Ray was stunned as well. He hadn't seen the boy since before his last stretch in prison. And he knew that now was a terrible time for a reunion.

Kitty pulled Timmy into the apartment. "Timmy," she told him. "Now be a good boy and have fun while you're staying with your father. I'll call you when I get back. Your dad'll put you on a bus back to Redding."

Kitty kissed Timmy on the cheek and hurried toward the door.

"Whoa, Kitty," Ray called, ignoring Timmy and chasing after his sister. "We gotta talk."

Timmy looked at Carl and Bobbie. "So . . . you ex-cons, too?" he asked pointedly.

Carl and Bobbie exchanged embarrassed glances.

Meanwhile, Ray stopped Kitty in the hallway and closed the door behind them.

"Seriously bad timing," he told her. "I can't have the kid around now."

"Look, Ray," said Kitty. "I've had Timmy for three years. *Three years*, Ray — "

"I know, I know. And I appreciate it — "

"So you can take him for a few days."

"But, I'm telling you," insisted Ray. "This is a *bad* time for me!"

"And I'm telling you," replied Kitty just as insistently. *"I'm going on my honeymoon!"*

A car horn blared from the street outside. Wayne was getting impatient.

"I gotta go," said Kitty as she retreated down the stairs. "Make sure he flosses. 'Bye, Ray. I'll be home Saturday."

Ray chased her across the landing. "Wait a minute!" he pleaded. "Where are you going? Can't you take him with you? Kitty!!!"

But by then Kitty was gone. Ray stood alone on the landing and pounded the banister in frustration.

4.
Unwanted

Minutes later Ray stood in the kitchen and watched as Timmy rummaged through the refrigerator looking for a snack.

"So, Tim," Ray began nervously. "Tim-boy, heh-heh. Look, unfortunately you've arrived at a — "

"June 1989?" Timmy read the expiration date off a jar of peanut butter. "I think this is expired. You better make a list. A shopping list. I'll need a few things."

Timmy pulled a pencil and spiral notebook out of his backpack and handed it to Ray.

"Okay, Jif peanut butter, crunchy style," he dictated as he scoped out the empty kitchen cupboards. "White bread. Don't get rye. I hate rye. Doritos, Cool Ranch flavor. Pepperidge Farm Double Chocolate Chip cookies. Count Chocula breakfast cereal. Oreos, Pepsi, and Häagen-Dazs strawberry ice cream. That should do it for starters."

Timmy noticed that Ray was not writing.

16

"Fine," he said. "I'll make the list." He took back the pencil and notebook and went into the living room.

"Guess I'll be crashing on the couch," he said. He began bouncing up and down on the couch cushions testing them for comfort. Carl and Bobbie grimaced with the knowledge that their robbery plans were just behind Timmy's back.

Ray followed Timmy into the living room. "Son, listen," he began.

But Timmy continued bouncing on the couch. "So what are we doing this week?" he asked his father. "I heard the aquarium's not bad. 'Course we gotta go to a Giants game. And I'd like to hit the Museum of Natural History."

"Timmy," Ray tried again. "We're not gonna —"

But Timmy whipped out a folded sheet of paper from his notebook. "I made an itinerary," he said. Carl scratched his head. He didn't know what an itinerary was. "That means a schedule of events," explained Timmy.

Then Timmy felt something brushing against his back. He reached around and pulled the rolled up plans from behind the cushion.

"What's this?" asked Timmy.

"None of your business," snapped Ray. He snatched the plans from Timmy's hands.

"What're you so nervous about?" asked Timmy suspiciously. "You got something to hide?"

Ray, Carl, and Bobbie looked at Timmy with their

best innocent expressions. "No. Nothing. 'Course not. Uh-uh," they mumbled over each other.

Timmy squinted his eyes at the three men. Something didn't seem right to him.

Ray turned to Carl and Bobbie. It was time to deal with Timmy head-on. "Give us a few minutes, will ya?" he asked his partners. Carl and Bobbie nodded and slipped off into the kitchen.

When they were alone Ray smiled at Timmy.

"I brought you something, Dad," said Timmy. He pulled a snapshot out of his backpack and handed it to Ray. "A picture of Mom and me." In it Timmy was in a cemetery standing next to the gravestone of his mother. On the gravestone was carved, BARBARA GLEASON, BORN OCT. 11, 1955, DIED JULY 10, 1989.

Ray was stunned by the photo. "It's . . . nice, Tim," he said politely and held it out to Timmy. "Real nice."

"Keep it," said Timmy. "I have others. You probably don't get to the grave too much, do you?"

Ray stared at him without saying a word.

"Didn't think so." Timmy noticed the dying elephant fern in the corner. "You should water that," he suggested.

Ray sat next to Timmy on the couch. "So, uh, how're you doing in school?" he asked.

"On my last Stanford Achievement Test, my overall scores rated me in the 95th percentile," Timmy said proudly.

"No kidding. And that's good?" Ray asked.

"It means that intellectually, I'm superior to ninety-five percent of the kids in my class."

"Whoa! That's *great!*" exclaimed Ray. There was a silence. Ray couldn't think of what to say next. "You dating yet?" he finally asked.

"I'm *eleven*," Timmy reminded his father.

"Yeah," agreed Ray. "It's good to wait. I didn't start dating till I was eleven and a half." He laughed. Timmy looked quizzically at Ray, not getting the joke.

"Well," Ray pressed on. "I'm glad we had this talk. We should do it more often. But not right now. You see, you picked a bad week to come, Tim. And I'm not going to be able to spend any time with you. I'm really swamped at work right now. At the bakery, you know I do cakes for them, I design cakes and we got *lots* of cakes this week, so you understand."

Timmy nodded solemnly at Ray, trying to hide his hurt feelings. He was finally beginning to realize that his own father didn't want him around.

"Kitty says you learned how to do that in prison," said Timmy. "Make cakes."

"Yeah," Ray nodded. "It was kind of a course I took. I *wanted* to get into the counterfeiting class but it was full up."

Again Ray waited for Timmy to laugh at his joke. Timmy just stared at him with a blank expression.

"What was prison like?" asked Timmy. "Did you ever try escaping?"

Ray shook his head. "Escaping? No. They kind of frown on that. They got signs posted and everything."

"Did you get my letters?"

Ray looked away from his son. He had gotten all of Timmy's letters.

"Why didn't you write back?" asked Timmy.

Ray shrugged. "I guess I didn't have much to say, Tim," he answered. "I mean, what am I gonna write? 'Having a wonderful time, wish you were here'?"

"You never even sent me a birthday card."

"Yeah, yeah, yeah," was all Ray could say. He was growing increasingly uncomfortable. He reached into his pocket and pulled out a twenty-dollar bill. "Look, I gotta discuss a few things with my friends, so here, take this money. There's a pizza place on the corner. Go on. Get whatever you want."

Timmy looked up at his father. At first he had thought that maybe this time things would be different. That this time maybe his father would be glad to see him. And would maybe want to do things with him.

He realized that he couldn't have been more wrong. He grabbed the twenty-dollar bill and headed down the hallway.

"Hey, where you going?" called Ray.

Timmy stopped. "If it's not too much to ask, *Dad*," he began sarcastically, "can I use your bathroom?" And with that he turned and went into the bathroom.

Timmy was about to close the door behind him when he heard voices from the living room.

"Ray, what is this?" came a voice. It was Bobbie, the nervous-looking one with the cigarette. There was something about him that Timmy didn't like. "You never told us you had a kid."

"So I forgot to tell you," he heard his father reply.

"Well whattaya gonna do with him?" Bobbie said. "He gets curious, he blows this — "

"Don't worry about it," came Ray's voice. "I'm stuck with him, but we'll work around it. He's just a kid. He's got no idea what's going on."

Upon hearing those words, Timmy closed the door behind him. He turned to the mirror and looked at his face. He saw his sad eyes and his hardened expression. He felt unwanted, unloved, in the way.

He decided right then that he would have to do something about that.

Timmy spent the night on the couch with a blanket wrapped around him. The next morning Ray awakened him.

"Timmy," said Ray. "I gotta go to work. I left some money there in case there's anything you wanna pick up at the market. You gonna be okay?"

Timmy didn't say anything. Instead, he stared coldly at his father.

Ray noticed the disappointment in Timmy's eyes. He tried to think of the right thing to say, but all he could come up with was, "Well, see ya. I'll be back late."

Timmy watched as his father grabbed an empty blue sports bag from the table.

"Stay outta trouble," said Ray just before leaving the apartment.

Timmy climbed off of the couch and walked to the window. He watched Ray get into his car and drive off. Seeing his father drive away like that reminded him of the last time he had seen Ray. He was only five years old at the time.

Then something happened that changed things forever. One day, while playing with his football on the front lawn, a police car drove up to their house. Two officers went into the house and arrested Ray. Later, after he had been put in the custody of Ray's sister, Timmy learned that his father had been convicted of grand larceny. Ray would be spending the next several years in prison.

That was the first time Timmy learned that his father was different from the other kids' fathers. *His* father was a crook. But Timmy didn't hold that against Ray. No matter what happened, Ray would always be his father. Timmy had hoped that Ray would feel the same.

Now he was beginning to have his doubts.

5.
Future Plans

Mr. Wankmueller was a kindly gentleman in his middle-seventies. He had been talking about selling his bakery from the first day Ray started working for him. For the last two years Ray had dreamed of being the one who would buy it. That morning Ray cornered Mr. Wankmueller in the bakery's back kitchen and rolled open some sketches he had drawn showing how he would expand the shop.

"I thought I'd knock out a wall there," Ray said, pointing to the inside wall of the kitchen. "And that's where I'd put the bagel operation."

"Bagels?" asked Mr. Wankmueller.

"Mr. Wankmueller," said Ray. "If you sell to me, not only do I continue the fine tradition of Wankmueller cakes, cookies, and breads, but I also give the public the highest quality Wankmueller bagel."

"*If* I sell," said Mr. Wankmueller as he mulled over Ray's ideas.

"You've been talking about doing that every day for the last two years," Ray reminded his boss. "And I got the financing already lined up."

Wankmueller looked up from the plans and smiled at Ray. "You're a good baker, Ray. But — "

"Look, Mr. Wankmueller," interrupted Ray. "I know I was a bum before you gave me a chance here. But I *know* I can make this place go. And if you sell to me, sir, you're not only selling to a good baker, you're selling to a guy who's now and forever a respectable, hardworking, one hundred percent law-abiding citizen."

Ray looked at Mr. Wankmueller with an expression that pleaded to be believed. At the same time, he was thinking ahead to the end of the day. That was the time he had arranged to meet Bobbie and Carl. The time when they would steal the coins from the Professional Coin Grading Service of San Francisco.

"Now I want everything going down smooth," Ray said to Bobbie and Carl. "Everything according to plan."

It was 4:30 P.M. The three men were driving through the busy streets of San Francisco in a van. They were on their way to the Professional Coin Grading Service. All were disguised, dressed in paint-splattered painter's overalls. All except Carl. His overalls were sparkling white.

"We're supposed to be painters," Ray commented to Carl. "You look like you're going on a space mission."

Carl shrugged. It didn't matter if they were on their way to steal a million-and-a-half-dollars' worth of coins. He wanted to look neat.

Ray pulled two small cylinders from his sports bag, both filled with cayenne pepper. He handed one to Bobbie and one to Carl. Rather than guns, the pepper spray would be their weapon.

As they drove along, Ray thought about Timmy. He had left the boy alone for the day. Now he wondered if that was the right thing to do. He was surprised when he first saw Timmy yesterday. The boy had grown so much. He was no longer the little tot he had once known. At eleven years old, Timmy was smart.

"You know my kid's in the 95th percentile?" Ray blurted out. Bobbie and Carl looked at him blankly. They had no idea what he was talking about.

Would Timmy be all right all alone? Ray wondered. Sure! He told himself. He's a smart kid. Practically all grown up. He can take care of himself just like his old dad. In fact, Ray found himself feeling proud of Timmy. The boy was turning out to be just like him.

Suddenly Ray paused in his thoughts.

He wondered, as the van approached the Professional Coin Grading Service of San Francisco, if being like him was anything to be proud of after all.

6.
The Concerned Citizen

Timmy was bored. He had spent the morning watching television, but the only things on were talk shows. Then, when he went to scope out something for breakfast, he remembered that his father's cupboard was completely bare.

He grabbed his camcorder and went out. He found a local diner and, with the twenty dollars his father had given him, ordered his breakfast: pancakes, bacon, and syrup, with three scoops of vanilla ice cream heaped on top.

Then he went for a walk in downtown San Francisco. He was nearing a bank when he saw an expensive-looking car parked in the handicapped spot of its parking lot. An important-looking man in a dark business suit got out of the car.

"Excuse me, sir," said Timmy, aiming his camcorder at the businessman. "I'm with Eyewitness News. The space you parked in is for handicapped drivers only. So I think you better move your car."

"Buzz off, ya' little creep," growled the businessman. He entered the bank.

Timmy quickly looked around until he saw a police car parked across the street at a donut shop. He went into the donut shop, found a policeman, and told him what he had just seen. The policeman followed Timmy to the bank parking lot and began writing out a ticket for the illegally parked car.

Just then the businessman came out of the bank.

"Hey, what is this?" he exclaimed.

"Looks like a twenty-two-five-oh-seven," explained the police officer. "Illegal parking in a handicap zone. And a thirty-three-twenty-six. Disobedience to signs."

"And the little tag on the license plate?" added Timmy. "It says ninety-one."

"That's an eight-oh-seven," explained the policeman. "Expired tags. Can I see your registration?"

"This is ridiculous!" said the businessman angrily. He hesitated. "I don't have it on me, okay? I think I lost it."

The police officer resumed writing in his ticket book. "No registration card: eight-oh-two. Well, let's see what we got here. A twenty-two-five-oh-seven, a thirty-three-twenty-six, an eight-oh-seven, and an eight-oh-two. Know what that adds up to?"

"Twenty - seven - thousand - four - hundred - and - forty-two!" announced Timmy happily.

"Exactly," said the policeman. He tore off the ticket and gave it to the businessman. "Thank God for concerned citizens, right, sir?"

The businessman threw a flustered look at Timmy.

"Well," said Timmy. "Better buzz."

And with that he proudly strolled away in search of something to do.

7.
The Heist

Bobbie stopped in front of the small office building where the Professional Coin Grading Service of San Francisco was located. Wearing a hardhat and carrying a toolbox, he looked like he belonged with the construction workers who were still emptying garbage into a Dumpster from the second floor of the building.

One of the workmen checked his watch and motioned to the others to quit work. When all the construction workers were gone, Bobbie nodded to Ray and Carl, who were a few feet away in the van.

The coast was clear.

Bobbie went into the building and pressed the button for the elevator. When the elevator doors opened, Bobbie hung a yellow OUT OF ORDER sign across the doorway. Then he went into the elevator and took out some tools.

He quickly rigged the elevator panel so it could

not be called to other floors. Then he began crossing some of its control wires.

So far, everything was going like clockwork.

Outside in the van, Ray and Carl waited. Carl was beginning to sweat. He was getting nervous. Finally he and Ray got out of the van. They were carrying paint cans, brushes, rollers — and Ray's sports bag. To anyone looking, they were just a couple of painters going to work. As soon as they entered the building, Ray pulled out a walkie-talkie and called Bobbie.

"We're in," he announced.

Bobbie was putting the finishing touches on the elevator control panel. He took out his walkie-talkie and answered, "Detour's wired."

Ray and Carl looked at the building directory. The Professional Coin Grading Service was on the top floor of the building. They found the stairwell, but only climbed to the second floor.

Ray looked out the hall window from the second floor. An armored car was pulling up to the building. Ray watched as two armed guards got out. Then he called Bobbie.

Upon getting the word that the armored car had arrived, Bobbie removed the OUT OF ORDER sign from the elevator. Then he quickly went into the next elevator and taped the sign to it.

When the two armed guards reached the elevator bank and noticed the OUT OF ORDER sign on one of the elevators they pressed the UP button and got into the elevator that Bobbie had rigged. They took the elevator to the top floor of the building and were let into the Professional Coin Grading Service office.

A company official loaded the now-famous hoard of slabbed coins into a metal carrying case. He locked the case and handed it to one of the armed guards. Then both guards left the office and got back into the elevator.

Waiting in the lobby, Bobbie watched the floor indicator over the elevator door and saw that the guards were taking the elevator back down. He switched on his walkie-talkie.

"Nonstop to you," he said to Ray. Then he left the building, his job done.

The elevator stopped on the second floor. The guards peeked out of the elevator to see what was going on, but all they saw were two painters busily painting the stairwell door.

The guards pressed the main floor button, but this time the elevator did not move.

"Let's walk down," said one of the guards.

The guards left the elevator and walked to the stairwell door where the painters were working. Just as they reached the door, however, the two painters turned on them. It was Ray and Carl. Carl raised his can of cayenne pepper and sprayed it into the eyes of the guards. The guards went down, choking and coughing. Carl and Ray took the guards' guns and dropped them into their buckets of paint. Then they pulled the guards into an empty office and tied and gagged them.

When the guards were safely tied up, Ray and Carl cut the coin case open with a power saw. Then they transferred the coins into Ray's sports bag.

"Charlie," Ray heard from one of the guard's walkie-talkies. It was a guard in the armored truck downstairs. "What's taking you guys so long? Charlie?"

Thinking fast, Ray grabbed the guard's walkie-talkie. "You mind?" he asked the waiting driver. "I'm in the bathroom!"

"Where's Mel?" asked the driver.

"He's in the bathroom, too," answered Ray.

"You both can't be in the bathroom," said the guard. "That's against regulations!"

In the armored truck, the waiting guard became very suspicious. "State your status," he ordered into his walkie-talkie. "State your status!" When his two partners did not reply, the waiting guard immediately turned on his dashboard mike and called for help.

Meanwhile, Ray and Carl zipped up the sports bag full of coins and ran down the hallway. Ahead of them was the Dumpster chute the construction workers had used to clear out their garbage. Ray and Carl jumped into the chute and slid out the side of the building.

At the same time Bobbie pulled the van up to the side of the building. Ray hit the ground and ran toward the van. Then he realized that Carl was not behind him. He turned and saw Carl dangling from the end of the dump chute, his overalls caught on its protruding edge.

"C'mon!" Ray shouted to Carl. "C'mon!"

"I'm stuck, Ray!" Carl cried out. His arms and legs were flailing helplessly.

WWWWRRRRR!

Police sirens, thought Ray. And they're getting closer!

Suddenly Carl's overalls ripped free of the chute. Carl fell into the Dumpster and disappeared into a cloud of dust. A second later he pulled himself up and over the side of the Dumpster and ran to the van.

Once Ray and Carl were safely inside the van, Bobbie stepped on the gas.

"No!" Ray ordered Bobbie. "Slow, slow. Take it easy."

Bobbie eased off on the gas and calmly cruised the van away from the building. Moving at that speed it didn't look like a getaway car. In fact, the van was hardly noticed by the two police cars that whipped past them on their way to the scene of the crime.

As soon as they were a safe distance away, Ray, Carl, and Bobbie sighed with relief. They had done it. They had actually stolen more than a million dollars' worth of valuable coins. Soon they would be rich men. They would be able to buy anything they wanted.

And they would be able to get respect.

8.
A Safe Hiding Place

Later that afternoon, after running out of things to do, Timmy returned to Ray's apartment. Ray was not home yet so Timmy sat himself down in front of the television set and began flicking through the channels with the remote control. That's when a late-breaking news bulletin caught his interest.

" — where this afternoon two armed guards were robbed of one and a half million dollars in rare coins," said the newscaster.

Timmy pressed a button on the remote, making the volume louder.

"The guards," continued the newscaster as video footage of the robbery scene flashed across the screen, "had just picked up the coins here from the Professional Coin Grading Service, when two men overpowered them on the second floor and made off with the coins."

Timmy thought for a moment. The news report reminded him of something, but he couldn't remember exactly what. Then it hit him.

He went into his father's bedroom. There on a bureau was Ray's copy of *The Numismatist Weekly*. Timmy had noticed the newspaper earlier. The headline that read COIN HORDE FOUND IN TRUNK was circled in red. Timmy read the article. It said the coins were "valued at $1.5 million."

"One point five million," Timmy said aloud. He was smart enough to know that that was the same as one *and a half* million.

Timmy was stunned. Now he knew why his father was too busy to spend time with him. And it wasn't because he had to design a special order of cakes at the bakery, either.

It was so he could pull off a robbery!

As soon as he could, Ray stopped off at a pay phone and called a man named Dobbs. Dobbs had promised to take the coins and, in exchange for a share, give Ray and his partners their cash value.

But Dobbs had a problem. He needed until Sunday to raise the cash. That was six days. Now Ray, Carl, and Bobbie had to figure out what to do with the coins until then.

They drove back to Ray's apartment.

Timmy heard the van pull up outside his window, so he looked out. He quickly got his camcorder and taped Ray, Carl, and Bobbie as they got out of the van. Ray was still carrying his sports bag, but it looked bulkier and heavier than it had that morning.

It was definitely filled with something, thought Timmy.

Timmy heard his father's footsteps climbing the hallway stairs. But instead of coming into the apartment, the footsteps continued on down the hall. Timmy ran to the door and opened it a crack. He peeped out. Ray was leading Carl and Bobbie through a door, that led to the roof. As soon as they went through the door, Timmy sneaked down the hall and followed them.

Timmy watched from the roof doorway. He stayed in the shadows, careful not to be seen. He watched as Ray used a screwdriver to remove some bricks from a barbecue pit that was built onto the side of a storage shed.

"How come we're hiding it at *your* place?" he heard Bobbie ask in a suspicious tone of voice.

" 'Cause no one's gonna find it here," replied Ray. "Nobody comes up here."

"Nobody comes up here?" challenged Bobbie. "You don't think *you'll* be tempted to come up and visit when we're not around? I want my share *now*, Ray. We split now."

"We can't split now," said Ray. "Every one of these coins is worth a different amount. When we get the money, *that's* when we split."

Timmy carefully cracked the roof door open for

a better look. The door let out a sharp squeak.

"Somebody's there!" exclaimed Bobbie. He headed straight for the door.

Timmy stumbled backward away from the door. Then he leaped behind some boxes under the stairs. Bobbie jerked the door open and looked in.

It seemed as if nobody was there after all.

"What'ja find there, Bob?" chuckled Ray. "Mike Wallace and the *60 Minutes* crew?"

By the time Bobbie returned, Ray had sealed up the barbecue pit. The coins were completely hidden from view.

"Safe as Fort Knox," said Ray confidently. "C'mon. Beers are on me."

Bobbie raised his hand. "Until we move that," he said, pointing to the hidden coins, "I'm watching you."

Ray stared at Bobbie. He was growing tired of his partner's suspicions.

"I better check on my kid," said Ray.

Bobbie smirked. "Sure," he said sarcastically. "The doting father. We'll wait."

Ray went back to his apartment while Bobbie and Carl waited in the hall. The TV was on and Timmy was on the couch fast asleep. Ray looked at his son for a moment. Asleep like that, Timmy looked like an innocent baby.

Certain that everything was under control, Ray left to join his friends.

As soon as he heard the door close, Timmy opened his eyes wide. He hadn't been asleep at all. He was just faking it, biding his time until the coast was clear.

And until he could start planning his revenge.

9.
Heisting from
the Heisters

The first thing Timmy did was watch Ray, Bob-
bie, and Carl from the living room window.
The three men got into the van and drove off.
Once he was certain that the coast was clear,
Timmy went to work.

He left the apartment and bolted upstairs to the
roof. It took a little strength, but he was able to
remove the bricks from the barbecue pit where
he had seen his father stash the sports bag.

Timmy reached in and pulled out the nylon bag.
He expected the bag to be heavier than it actually
was. Instead, it seemed light. Had he been wrong
about his father? He hoped so. But when he
opened the bag, his suspicions were confirmed. It
was filled with a bunch of coins. There were not
as many as he expected, and he wondered how so
little could be worth so much.

Next, he carried the coins back down to the
apartment and spread them out on the kitchen
table. Turning on his camcorder he videotaped

them. He made sure to use the same tape he had used when he taped his father coming home from the robbery earlier that evening.

Finally, he wrapped the videotape in a mailing envelope. After addressing the envelope he went outside and dropped it into a mailbox. Once that was done, Timmy had one more errand to run. He took his father's blue bag, got on a cable car to a secret place, and hid the bag. Then he went back home, sat down in front of the television set, and waited patiently for his father to come home.

While Timmy waited, Ray and Carl were drinking beers at a nearby bar. They were feeling pretty good about things, talking about what they were going to do with their share of the loot.

"Hey, where's Bobbie?" asked Carl. Bobbie had excused himself earlier. He had been gone for quite some time.

Ray got suspicious and went into the men's room. There he saw Bobbie on top of the toilet trying to sneak out the small bathroom window.

"Going somewhere, Bob?" Ray asked him.

Bobbie was startled. He slipped off the toilet.

"I was going for my share of the coins, okay?" he answered. "That's all I want. *My* share!"

"How many times I gotta tell you," explained Ray. "We can't split the coins up until Dobbs cashes 'em in!"

"We can split 'em three ways and when Dobbs comes, we bring our stashes together," said Bobbie. "Then we split the cash even. Do it my way, or you're gonna have to worry every time I get up and leave the room, Ray."

And with that Bobbie stormed back into the bar. Ray stayed behind thinking. His perfect plan was unraveling. Something would have to be done, something that would put Bobbie's suspicions to rest.

When they were done with their beers Ray brought Carl and Bobbie back to the roof of his apartment building.

"Okay," began Ray. "Each of us reaches into the bag and grabs a coin. We do this till they're all gone. And I don't want anyone complaining about what coin they get, 'cause it's all by chance."

Bobbie and Carl nodded eagerly. They had all agreed that this was the only way to make certain each one of them got their fair share. But when Ray leaned over the barbecue pit to remove the loosened bricks he noticed that it had already been moved. He shoved his arm into the barbecue pit.

"It's gone," he said, starting to panic.

"Gone?" moaned Bobbie. "GONE?"

Ray quickly began to remove some of the other bricks from the barbecue pit. But no matter how many he removed he couldn't find the sports bag full of coins.

"Excuse me, guys," came a voice from across the roof. Ray, Bobbie, and Carl turned their heads. It was Timmy. "I think we better talk."

Twenty minutes later Ray, Bobbie, and Carl were seated around the kitchen table waiting impatiently for Timmy to swallow a mouthful of a peanut butter sandwich he had made for himself.

Timmy swallowed, took a big drink of milk, and sighed with satisfaction.

Then he explained that he had figured out that they had stolen the coins . . . and that he could prove it. "After I raided your hiding place, I spread the coins here on the table and videotaped them with my camera," Timmy said. "I also got some good shots of you coming into the building, so I'm sure the cops will have no trouble identifying you."

"What are you trying to pull, you little weasel!" shouted Bobbie angrily. He lunged at Timmy, but Ray held him back.

"*Bob*," he said, warning his partner not to hurt his son. Bobbie sat back down, fuming.

"Go on, Tim," Ray said to his son calmly.

"That videotape," continued Timmy, "is on its way to a friend of mine, along with a letter that tells the whole story."

The three men were dumbfounded. They

watched helplessly as Timmy took another bite out of his peanut butter sandwich.

"Okay, Tim. You got us," said Ray good-naturedly. He was hoping Timmy was only pulling an elaborate prank. "Right, guys? Let's admit it. He's got us."

Carl joined in laughing. Bobbie just glared tight-lipped at Timmy.

"So," continued Ray. "The coins, Tim. *Where* are the coins?"

"Wouldn't *you* like to know," replied Timmy.

Bobbie jumped out of his chair again. "That cuts it!" he yelled at the boy. "When I sassed my old man, he took his belt to me — the *same thing* I'm gonna do to you!"

Ray jumped up and pushed Bobbie back into his seat. Timmy scrambled behind his father.

"Hold on, Bob!" ordered Ray.

"Lemme go, Ray! I'll get the little creep to talk!"

"I said hold on," repeated Ray. "Nobody's hurting anyone here!"

"That's right," said Timmy, peeking out from behind his father. "Because if *anything* happens to me — if I don't call my friend every night and give him a *new* password, he's taking that video straight to the cops. And you'll *all* go to prison for a long, long time!"

"Okay, Tim," Ray said calmly. He was hoping to reason with the boy. "I haven't exactly been the model father. You're angry, I understand. But I still *am* your father. And I know you'd never rat on your own flesh and blood."

"Just try me," said Timmy. He was deadly serious.

Ray, Carl, and Bobbie exchanged frustrated glances. Timmy meant business.

"I'm looking for the coins," declared Bobbie.

Bobbie began rifling through the kitchen cabinets, tossing out pots and pans and emptying boxes of food. Carl checked the hall closets and wastebaskets throughout the apartment. Ray went downstairs and checked the basement and the laundry room. Then he went outside and checked the Dumpster behind the building.

During all this, Timmy sat in the living room and watched cartoons.

An hour had gone by. Ray, Carl, and Bobbie had turned the apartment upside down. No coins.

"Okay, Tim," Ray said, giving in. "You've had your fun. But now I want to know. What do you want?"

"He wants in on the deal, that's what," Bobbie said to Ray between clenched teeth. "But he's not getting any of my share. He's your kid, you split with him."

"I don't want any money," said Timmy. "I think stealing is wrong."

"You think stealing is wrong?" asked Bobbie. *"Then why'd you steal the coins from us?"*

"You've got this all wrong, Tim," said Ray. "Do you know who those coins belong to?"

"Well, me right now," answered Timmy.

"They don't belong to anybody," explained Ray. "They used to belong to an old lady, but she died and the government, the state, confiscated 'em. They *stole* 'em, Tim. So now they're gonna sell 'em, and you know where the money goes? To buy limousines for fat-cat politicians, that's where. Now, what am I gonna do with the money? I'm buying the bakery where I work, Tim. I'm gonna expand, hire more people. Those people will pay taxes. Eventually, the government gets its money back. And your dad's got a respectable business, he's through with crime. He's *straight.*"

Timmy looked at his father, mulling over the explanation. "So you're saying," he said, "you want to go straight and to do that you have to steal."

Ray nodded, a little embarrassed at the way it sounded.

"I'm eleven," said Timmy. "And that seems dumb even to me."

"I say we hang him off the roof by his ankles," snarled Bobbie. "Let's vote."

This time Ray didn't argue with Bobbie. He, too, was losing his patience.

"So tell me what you want," he asked Timmy.

"Ever since I got here, you've ignored me," answered his son.

"I was planning a robbery, son," replied Ray. Then he exploded. *"What'd you expect me to do. Take you camping?"*

Timmy quickly pulled a slip of paper from his pocket and unfolded it. "You know what I want?" he said, handing the paper to Ray. "I want *this*."

Ray looked at the slip of paper. It was a list of activities written in Timmy's handwriting.

"What is this?" asked Ray. "The aquarium? The Giants game? The museum? You want to go to all these places?"

"I want *you* to take me," explained Timmy. "I want you to pretend you like having me around for the week. And if you do real good, Dad, I'll tell you where the coins are."

Timmy climbed off the couch and stretched. "Well, I'm turning in," he said with a yawn. "I'll be sleeping in your bed. *You* take the couch."

Timmy marched into his father's bedroom and closed the door behind him.

Ray, Carl, and Bobbie looked at each other helplessly. They felt pretty stupid. They had spent weeks planning the biggest heist of their careers. They pulled the job without a hitch. They were close to being wealthy beyond their wildest dreams.

And they were being blackmailed by an eleven-year-old.

10.
The Cops

Detective Theresa Walsh, twenty-eight years old, careened the unmarked police car toward the crime scene. On the street in front of her a team of police officers was examining the body of a murder victim. Beside her in the car was her partner, Detective Alex Ceranski. He winced and grabbed the dashboard as she brought the car to a jerky stop.

"Did too!" Ceranski said to Theresa, continuing the argument they had been having ever since the last intersection.

"I did *not!*" replied Theresa insistently.

"Walsh," said Ceranski. "You came this close to hitting the cable car. Gee whiz, you're already on probation for shooting your last partner in the foot. You trying to get rid of me with a heart attack?"

"How many times you gotta bring that up?" replied Theresa. "I told you: My gun discharged. It was an accident. And if you want to drive from now on, here, take the keys. Be my guest."

Theresa threw the keys at her partner and abruptly got out of the car. Ceranski watched her as she moved toward the crime scene. She had on her usual conservative gray suit and her hair was pulled back in its usual tight bun. Although he liked her enthusiasm, he felt that she tried too hard at being a cop and not hard enough at being a person. Then he smiled. She reminded him of himself, years earlier, when he was just starting out.

Theresa stormed past the bustling police activity and approached a plainclothes officer who was eating a banana. It was her boss, Lieutenant Romayko. He was surprised to see her.

"Oh, Lieutenant," said Theresa. "Sir, we may have a lead on that coin robbery."

"Is that so, Walsh?" he said as he pulled back more of his banana peel. "Tell me, did you happen to notice that this was a crime scene?"

Theresa looked around her. "Well," she said. "Yes, sir."

"And MacReady, what's the most important thing at a crime scene?"

"Evidence," answered Lieutenant MacReady, a woman police detective several years older than Theresa.

"Evidence, exactly," said Lieutenant Romayko. "And you know what you just did, Walsh?" He pointed to the ground with his banana. "You just ran over evidence."

Theresa looked down and grimaced. Behind her front tire, lying in a chalk circle, was the shell casing of a bullet, now crushed. Romayko picked it up and held it carefully by its edges.

"Now how are we going to match this shell casing to the murder weapon?" Romayko asked Theresa.

Theresa slumped her shoulders. "Oh, gee," she stammered. "I'm — I'm very sorry, sir."

By now Ceranski had gotten out of the car and joined them. He rolled his eyes with embarrassment.

"Lucky we found some other casings," said Romayko. "But for somebody already on probation, I'd think you'd be a little more careful, Walsh. Ceranski, you drive from now on."

"That's already been arranged," said Ceranski, dangling the car keys.

"Good," said Romayko. "And, Walsh — " he handed her his empty banana peel. "Take care of this."

Romayko and MacReady stormed off and returned to the business of examining the crime scene. Theresa looked dejected. She felt as if all she ever did was make mistakes.

"Hey," said Ceranski. "At least you didn't run over the body."

Theresa, not cheered by Ceranski's joke, threw a stern glance at him as she returned to their car.

That afternoon Theresa and Ceranski gathered

in Lieutenant Romayko's office. Theresa had said she had some new evidence in the coin robbery and Romayko wanted to see it. Theresa pushed a tape into the Lieutenant's VCR and the three of them watched as a police detective interrogated a gaunt-looking man in a trenchcoat. The man looked as if he hadn't eaten in days. He smoked a cigarette and wheezed when he talked.

"So you were out in the alley and you heard two men arguing in the rest room about splitting their share of the coins," the police officer on the tape asked the man.

"Yep," the man said in a raspy voice. Then he let out a hacking cough.

"And you're sure their names were Ray and Bob?" continued the police officer.

"Yep," wheezed the man. "Bob and Ray. You know, like those guys used to be on radio? Whatever happened to them? They were funny."

"And you think their fence was someone named Dobbs?" the police officer asked.

"Yep," answered the man. "Now what about my money? You said I get fifty bucks for — "

Romayko clicked off the TV set. He and Ceranski looked warily at Theresa.

"*This* is our informant?" Ceranski asked his partner. "Some guy from Winos-R-Us?"

"That true, Walsh?" added Romayko. "This is your 'lead'?" Romayko had several bottles of vitamins and stress pills on his desk. He now began to take one pill from each bottle and swallow it.

"But I do have something," said Theresa. "I think."

Romayko swallowed another pill. "Can we hear it before my arteries harden?" He was becoming impatient.

"Yes, sir," responded the rookie detective. "Based on what the wino said, I cross-checked the names of local perpetrators who've worked together in the past. I came up with these two. Bobbie Drace and Ray Gleason."

Theresa handed folders to Ceranski and Romayko. Inside were mug shots and rap sheets of Bobbie and Ray.

"Grand theft, mail fraud," Romayko read Ray's rap sheet aloud.

"Some penny-ante stuff," concluded Ceranski with skepticism. "C'mon. Some juicer thinks he hears a couple names and — "

"I also did some checking through NCIC," added Theresa. "There've been four major coin robberies in the last two years. Each time, an auction house or coin grading company was hit."

Ceranski raised his eyebrows. "You're saying *these* clowns are behind these jobs?"

"No, but what if 'Dobbs' is? He's gotta be the specialist to move the stuff, right? Maybe he sets it all up, finds local talent to do the job. If these *are* the guys, then they're waiting for him, sir. This could be our break to solve *all* these cases."

Ceranski and Romayko exchanged looks. They were still unconvinced.

"All I'm saying is," Theresa plowed on, "if we pick up Gleason and Drace now, we'll scare off Dobbs. *But* if we put 'em on twenty-four-hour surveillance, and wait for Dobbs to show, we can nail 'em *all*."

"Okay," said Romayko. "I'll give you a few days. But you better come up with something."

Theresa smiled. Ceranski looked as if he were about to groan.

"You look like you're going to pop a cork, Ceranski," Romayko noticed. "You got something to add?"

Ceranski shook his head. "No, no, sir," he answered. "The rookie's got it all figured out. I'm just the driver." Then he threw Theresa a flustered look and walked out of the office.

"Walsh," Romayko said when Ceranski was gone. "The fact that I was good friends with your father — it won't cut you any slack. Your probation report is coming up, so don't blow this."

Theresa thought of her father. He had been a good cop in his day. The hardest thing was living up to his image in the eyes of the older officers who knew him. Being a woman seemed to make it even harder.

"I won't, sir," Theresa promised solemnly.

11.
The Timmy Gleason Dream Vacation Begins

The next morning, Theresa and Ceranski were parked outside of Ray's apartment building. They had been there for an hour when they saw a little blond-haired boy emerge.

"C'mon, c'mon!" shouted Timmy as he bounded down the apartment building steps. "The day's a-wasting!"

Timmy raced toward Ray's car, his backpack bouncing about his shoulder.

Seconds later, Ray, Bobbie, and Carl emerged from the building.

"Who's the kid?" asked Ceranski.

Theresa seemed confused. "I don't know," she answered. Then she pulled out her camera and began taking snapshots of Ray, Bobbie, and Carl.

"You don't have to come along, you know," Ray said to his partners. They were unaware that they were being watched.

"Oh, no?" Bobbie replied suspiciously. "Listen,

56

'Dad': He tells you where the coins are, *I'm* gonna be there to hear it."

"Me, too, Ray," added Carl, though he was kind of looking forward to the idea of spending the day at the aquarium.

The three men followed Timmy to the car.

Ray opened the car door. Inside, old candy wrappers and newspapers were strewn about. It was filthy.

"Maid's day off, Dad?" quipped Timmy as his father cleaned off the seats.

Soon, everyone was inside the car. Timmy turned to Bobbie and Carl, who were in the backseat.

"Okay," he told them. "Here are the rules. If you're coming along, you have to join in *all* the activities. Okay?"

"Sure, kid," sneered Bobbie. "We got it."

"Seat belts," ordered Timmy. He fastened his own, but nobody else moved. "It's the *law*, isn't it?" he insisted.

The three men reluctantly began to fasten their seat belts.

"We do a boost worth a million-five, but *we* gotta worry about the seat-belt law," groaned Bobbie.

"And could you put that out, please?" Timmy asked Bobbie. Bobbie had been smoking a cigarette. "Your smoke bothers me."

"I don't care if my smoke *poisons* you," Bobbie snapped back.

"Bob," said Ray. "Douse it."

So Bobbie, fuming and muttering under his breath, jammed the cigarette into the ashtray.

Timmy smiled. "We can go now," he said.

Ray drove to the San Francisco Aquarium. Theresa and Ceranski followed close behind.

"The aquarium?" asked Theresa. "What're they doing here?"

"Could be robbing the place," laughed Ceranski. "Any second now they'll come running out with a porpoise under each arm."

"Or they could be meeting their contact," Theresa suggested without smiling. "I'm going in."

Theresa put on a scarf and sunglasses.

"What is that you're doing?" asked Ceranski. Theresa threw a cold stare at him. "Oh," he realized. "A *disguise*. Very effective. They won't spot you. Noooooo."

Theresa ignored Ceranski's sarcastic remark, got out of the car, and followed Ray, Carl, Bobbie, and Timmy into the aquarium.

"Hey! Fish!" noticed Carl.

"It's an aquarium, chucklehead," smirked Bobbie. "What'd you expect? Giraffes?"

"Look!" shouted Timmy. "They're feeding the sharks!"

Timmy ran off to a large tank. A group of sharks

were clambering for the food that a tank attendant was throwing to them.

"I wish *he* was the main course," Bobbie grumbled as he watched Timmy enjoy himself.

Then Timmy walked up to another tank, pulled his camcorder out of his backpack and began taping. Inside the tank was a long, thin fish with a sharp, pointy face. When he finished shooting he noticed that Ray was standing beside him.

"If you were a fish," Timmy asked his father, "what kind of fish would you be?"

"Gee, I don't know," answered Ray. "A porpoise maybe?"

"A porpoise isn't a fish, it's a mammal."

"All right, all right," Ray said. He felt dumb. Then he gestured to the wolf eel. "How 'bout this guy? Wolf eel. Bet nobody messes with him."

"It's not really an eel, Dad," explained Timmy. "I'm studying about the ocean in school."

"That's nice, Tim," said Ray. "But the sign says Wolf Eel. I think the people who put up these signs know what they're talking about."

"Dad, is a sea horse a horse?"

"Well, no. But — "

"Is a prairie dog a dog? And how about the L.A. Lakers? There are no lakes in Los Angeles. Why would they name their basketball team the Lakers?"

Ray had a dumbfounded look on his face. It was

clear he did not know the answers.

"I rest my case," said Timmy. Then he moved to the next tank. Ray followed. The sign on the tank said the creature inside was called a cuttlefish.

"But it's not a fish, Dad," explained Timmy, as Ray read the name plaque.

"It is so a fish," said Ray. "It says so right there. Cuttlefish."

Just then a group of schoolkids about Timmy's age approached the cuttlefish tank. They were with a tour guide who had overheard Timmy and Ray's discussion.

"He's right, children," said the tour guide. Then, gesturing to Timmy and Ray, she said, "Please, continue."

Ray smiled. He knew he had been right about the cuttlefish. Maybe he wasn't so dumb after all. "Well, thank you," he said to the tour guide. "Like I was saying — "

"No, not you," the tour guide interrupted. "Him." She pointed to Timmy.

Ray's shoulders slumped with embarrassment.

"It's no big thing really," said Timmy. "As I was trying to explain to my father, the cuttlefish is actually a relative of the octopus. It's a cephalopod, not a fish."

"Very good," said the tour guide, very impressed with Timmy. She turned to Ray. "You must be very proud of him."

Ray's lips turned up in a half smile. "Proud ain't the word," he said, red-faced. Then, as if to show the children that he wasn't completely stupid, he pointed to the previous tank and said: "By the way, that wolf eel over there? It's not really an eel."

But by that time the tour guide had led the school group away.

Ray turned to Timmy. A smirk was on his son's face.

"Okay, okay," he began. "So how'd you get so smart?"

"Beats me," answered Timmy. "Sure doesn't run in the family."

Timmy walked off. Ray just stood there, bristling. Things didn't seem to be going the way he wanted. It was his job to "play dad," to gain Timmy's confidence so that the boy would tell him where the coins were hidden.

But Timmy was smarter than he thought and he wasn't sure how he felt about that. Should he be angry — or proud?

"How're you getting along with him, Ray?" asked Carl as he approached Ray from behind.

"Terrific!" Ray exclaimed with faked confidence. "By the end of today he'll be in the palm of my hand!"

Ray and his two partners followed Timmy out of the aquarium.

"That was fun," said Timmy gleefully. "Next I thought we'd all go to Alcatraz."

The three men stopped dead in their tracks. Alcatraz was a famous prison. And they had all been to prison once before — as inmates.

"Maybe that's not such a good idea," agreed Timmy. Ray, Bobbie, and Carl sighed and followed Timmy to the parking lot.

Theresa had been following them since they entered the aquarium. Try as she might, she couldn't figure out what three felons were doing following a little boy.

She decided that before the day was over she would radio headquarters and find out just who that little boy was.

12.
Playing Dad

After leaving the aquarium, Theresa and Ceranski tailed their suspects to an indoor ice-skating rink. They watched as Timmy glided across the ice with his camcorder, taping his father and the others as they clumsily tried to keep up with him.

Ceranski watched them from the snack bar. After a few minutes, Theresa entered the building and joined him.

"Who is that kid?" Ceranski asked.

"He's Gleason's son," answered Theresa. She had just called headquarters and learned that Ray Gleason had a son who fit the description of the little boy. "It couldn't be the other two," she added. "He's a good-looking kid."

Ceranski caught the look on Theresa's face as she watched Ray pick himself up from the ice a second time. Ceranski could tell that Theresa thought Ray was handsome. It was not the way a cop should look at a suspect and it made Ceranski feel very uncomfortable.

Next stop was Candlestick Park. Theresa and Ceranski followed their suspects into the baseball stadium and sat a few rows behind them in the bleachers. Theresa spied on them through a pair of binoculars.

It was Bat Day. Directly behind Timmy and the others sat a kids' baseball team. Each player looked to be about Timmy's age. Like Timmy, they each held a baseball bat. Each time the home team made a play the kids jumped up and cheered.

One of them kept hitting Bobbie in the back of his head with a bat.

"Watch it with that bat, kid!" growled Bobbie. "That's the second time you hit me!"

With that, the kids' coach told them to pass their bats down the aisle. He leaned them up against the side of his seat.

"We gotta come on Bat Day," grumbled Bobbie. "Ten thousand kids with lethal weapons. What's next? Meat cleaver day? Uzi day?"

Timmy frowned. Bobbie was making it hard for him to have fun. "Do they have to come everywhere with us?" he whispered to his father.

"No," answered Ray. "Just tell me where you hid the stuff and they'll go away. It'll be just you and me."

"If I told you where it is, then you wouldn't take me anywhere."

"Sure I would," insisted Ray. "You gotta trust me. Give me a chance."

Timmy thought for a moment. "The reason they're sticking with us," he reasoned, "is because they think I'll tell *you* where the stuff is, but you won't tell *them*. If they don't trust you, why should I?"

Ray tapped his fingers on his bleacher seat. "You're starting to get on my nerves," he said.

Just then Carl returned from the snack bar with a box of goodies. Bobbie grabbed the box and began rummaging through it.

"Where's my ice-cream sandwich?" he demanded.

"Under the hot dogs," answered Carl.

Bobbie reached deep into the box and pulled out something in a cold, but soggy, wrapper. "Terrific," he sighed. "It's melted. What kind of brain-dead moron puts ice cream under hot dogs! Fine. I'll get my own."

Bobbie rose from his seat and squeezed his way down the row, grumbling. As he reached the end of the aisle the entire audience cheered when a Giants batter hit one out of the park. Bobbie turned to look at the ball field, but didn't notice that he knocked into Timmy's Bat Day bat, which was sticking out into the aisle. The bat slid backward into the stack of bats the kids' team's coach had piled together in the aisle of the next row.

SPLAT! The pile of bats spread out on the steps behind Bobbie. Then Bobbie turned around. His foot landed on the pile of bats. The bats rolled under his feet. Bobbie began flailing his arms, desperately trying to hold onto his balance. But soon his feet went flying up over his head and he tumbled head over heels down the cement steps and landed at the bottom of the bleachers with a thud.

Bobbie raised his head painfully. "Bat Day," he groaned.

"Palm of your hand, Ray?" Bobbie asked accusingly. He remembered what Ray had said at the aquarium. *"Palm of your hand?"*

They had gone back to Ray's apartment after the ball game. Bobbie was lying on the couch with an ice pack on his head. Ray and Carl were sitting across from him.

"Hey, I'm doing the best I can here," Ray said in his own defense. "Don't worry, we take him to a few more places, he'll loosen up."

"He better," warned Bobbie. "Or the next time you see his face will be on a milk carton."

From the living room the men could hear Timmy in the kitchen talking to his friend on the telephone.

"The password for today is 'bogus,' " they heard

Timmy say. "Get that Jason? Yeah, I'm having an *excellent* time. Remember, I'll call you every night with a new password. And if I don't, you take that video straight to the cops. 'Bye, Jason."

Timmy hung up the phone and then popped his head into the living room.

"Better get your sleep, guys," he suggested to the three men. "We got another *biiiiig* day to-morrow."

The next day Timmy directed his father to an amusement park. Once at the park, Timmy forced Ray, Bobbie, and Carl to take him on every ride.

First there was the roller coaster. Then there were the bumper cars. These were followed by rides with names like *Whiplash*, *Shock Wave*, *Panic Attack*, *Death Trap*, and finally, *Exterminator*.

By the time they had finished the rides the three men were white-knuckled and dizzy.

But Timmy loved every minute of it. For the first time since he could remember, he was having fun with his father.

The next day they went fishing. Timmy and Ray sat along the shoreline of a lake casting fishing lines into the water. But try as he might, Timmy was only able to cast his line a few feet out.

"Hasn't anyone taught you how to cast before?" asked his father.

"No," replied Timmy. "My father was usually in jail."

Ray decided to ignore the stinging remark. Instead, he stood behind Timmy and clamped his hand over the boy's hand on the pole handle.

"Like this," he said, demonstrating. "Back at one o'clock and — " Ray snapped his wrist forward and made a good deep cast out into the water.

"Did your dad teach you that?" asked Timmy, impressed.

"No, Tim," answered Ray. "He didn't." He was remembering his own father and how little time they had spent together when he was a child.

"I guess your family was dysfunctional, too," said Timmy. "That's what we are, you and me. We're dysfunctional."

Ray grinned. "You been watching too many talk shows," he quipped, even though he suspected that Timmy was right.

A few feet down the shore Carl was also casting a line out into the water. Bobbie was behind him pacing angrily back and forth.

"Only one way to handle this," Bobbie said to himself. "Only one way. I gotta get that kid alone. Just once. Then I'll make that kid talk."

Just then Carl whipped his pole back to cast. But when he tried pulling the pole forward it didn't follow through. Suddenly he heard Bobbie scream. He turned. His hook had gotten caught in Bobbie's earlobe.

"We're dysfunctional," remarked Timmy upon seeing this. "But they're stupid."

After lunch, Ray followed Timmy's instructions and took him to a park that had a batting practice cage. Using the bat he had got at Candlestick Park, Timmy stood in the front of the batting cage and began swinging at baseballs. He wasn't very good at it. In fact, he missed every pitch.

"You're uppercutting," Ray coached from the side. "Level swing. Watch the ball hit the bat."

For the next pitch Timmy concentrated. He followed the ball with his eyes and made a clean hit. He smiled. When he looked up he saw that Ray was smiling, too. Even Carl, who was behind the batting cage eating a hog dog, was smiling.

The only one who wasn't smiling was Bobbie. He stood off to the side, his head still aching from Bat Day, his fish-hooked earlobe taped and bandaged. He impatiently lit another cigarette and marched over to Ray.

"You know what I think?" Bobbie asked Ray. "I think you're starting to *like* playing dad. That's what I think!"

Ray pulled Bobbie to the side, out of earshot of Timmy.

"Listen," he insisted. "I'm just doing what the kid wants. I'm playing my role, Bob. Why don't you calm down, go home, and drink some warm milk. You look terrible."

"That's what you'd like, isn't it?" Bobbie replied. He was squinting his eyes with suspicion. "Get me outta the way so you and Carl can have the coins to yourself!"

Ray plucked the cigarette out of Bobbie's mouth. "Filtered cigarettes, Bob," he commented. "The lack of nicotine is causing brain fade. Better go back to the hard stuff."

And with that, Ray broke the filter off and stuck the cigarette back into Bobbie's mouth. Bobbie just glared at him and walked away.

Ray returned to Timmy and continued to coach him on his swing. He had to continue to "play his role" until Timmy told him where the money was hidden. The funny thing was that, before Bobbie interrupted the practice, Ray had forgotten about the money.

He even forgot that he was playing dad.

13.
Timmy's Game

Miniature golf was next on Timmy's list of things to do. The golf course was filled with families. All around him Timmy could see fathers and mothers and sons and daughters hitting golf balls. To him it was the perfect place to hang out with your dad — even if your dad's two friends were kind of geeks.

"How 'bout we make this interesting?" Timmy asked his three escorts as they approached the first tee on the miniature golf course.

"Just hit the ball you little rodent," Bobbie said. "I'm tired of your stupid games."

"I was just going to say that if anybody beats me, I'll tell you where the coins are. But if you don't want me to do that — "

Ray, Bobbie, and Carl exchanged surprised glances.

"Hold it, hold it," said Ray. "Are you saying if any one of us beats you, you tell us where the — "

"That's what I said," interrupted Timmy. "And if *I* win — "

"What?" groaned Bobbie. "What? We gotta take you to Paris tonight?"

"No." Timmy smiled. "Baskin-Robbins."

The men looked at each other. It was almost *too* easy. "You're on!" all three exclaimed at once.

From then on the men took their miniature golf game very seriously. They cheered loudly and high-fived each other when they made a putt. They groaned and cursed when they missed one.

Timmy coolly made one long putt after another. Maybe he couldn't cast the best fishing line in the world, but golf was definitely *his* game.

Ray watched as his son easily scored putt after putt through the windmill hole, the castle hole, and the overpass bridge hole. He was impressed. He even felt proud.

Hole four was a little red schoolhouse. Bobbie hit the ball up the incline, but it rolled back down. Carl gestured Bobbie back, straightened his tie and walked up to the tee. He took a mighty swing and smashed the ball. The ball rocketed up and smashed the window of the little schoolhouse.

Nearly an hour later, things weren't looking so good for Ray, Bobbie, and Carl. Ray had missed the clown's mouth at hole seven, and it took Bobbie six tries to get the ball into the windmill hole. Now Carl was preparing to hit the ball at a pirate ship.

"Try to hit your ball in there," Timmy said to Carl. "Through the center of the pirate ship. When pirates buried stuff they stole, you know how they found it later? They had a treasure map."

"Uh-huh," said Carl. He wasn't really listening. He was lining up his shot. Then he pulled back his golf club and gently putted. The ball rolled directly through the center of the model ship.

"I did it!" Carl exclaimed happily.

Bobbie walked over to Timmy. "Now it's the lad's turn," he said snidely. "Don't be nervous, son."

Timmy put his ball down onto the tee. As he swung his club at it, Bobbie bent over and cleared his throat loudly into Timmy's ear. Timmy jolted. His ball ricocheted off the pirate ship and into a pond.

Bobbie smiled. "Let's see," he said. "One stroke, another for going into the water. You're hitting *three* now, laddie."

Timmy looked up at Ray with a disappointed expression. Bobbie was *cheating*. Ray looked away, embarrassed.

The next hole was the last. Ray had managed to get his ball only five feet from the cup. If he could sink the ball he would win the game. Timmy would have to tell him where the money was hidden.

Ray bent over his ball. He was concentrating very hard.

"Make that and you win, Dad," said Timmy. "Just think how much this putt is worth. All that money."

"Shut up, kid!" yelled Bobbie. "If you're trying to psyche him out, it won't work!"

"Easy stroke, Ray," Carl said reassuringly. "You can do it."

Ray gently tapped the ball. It inched its way toward the cup, rolled around its rim, then rolled away.

Bobbie dropped to his knees, pounded the ground with his fist and started crying like a baby.

"No! No! Noooooooo!" he wailed. "We were *that* close! *That* close!"

Timmy turned to Ray. His father was standing at the cup, stunned at having lost the game.

"I guess I've improved since the last time we played," said Timmy. "You probably don't remember."

"Your fifth birthday," said Ray. "I took you and nine other little boys for miniature golf and pizza. Compared to that day, prison was a picnic."

Timmy's face broke into a smile. Ray smiled, too. He liked the way his son looked when he smiled. He looked innocent. Almost the way Ray remembered him when he was five years old. He used to be able to make Timmy smile a lot in those days.

Timmy and Ray looked at each other for a long moment.

"Well, c'mon," said Ray as he turned to walk away. "You want ice cream or not?"

A big smile spread across Timmy's face. He followed Ray out of the park.

14.
The Treasure Map

"**O**ne lousy little putt," said Bobbie, as he and Carl followed Timmy and Ray through the miniature golf course parking lot. "*Why* did it come out? *Why?* Well, I'll tell you this: I'm through being pushed around by that kid. Through!"

"Treasure map," mumbled Carl. Bobbie stopped. It looked like Carl was remembering something important. " 'When pirates buried their treasure they made a map.' The kid said it while we were playing. Something about a treasure map."

"Treasure map?" Bobbie asked. "You think he — ?"

"Made a map to where the coins are!" finished Carl. He felt pretty smart just then. "We gotta tell Ray — "

"No," said Bobbie, lowering his voice. "We keep this to ourselves. We check it out first. *Don't* tell Ray."

Later, when they were all in the car on the way to the nearest Baskin-Robbins, Bobbie told Ray to drop him and Carl off at the apartment. They weren't in the mood for ice cream. Ray was suspicious.

"What have you guys got going?" he asked as he pulled the car up in front of his apartment building. Bobbie and Ray got out.

"Nothing, Ray," said Bobbie. "Just gonna hang around here. Watch some TV. You don't mind, do you?"

"C'mon, Dad," said Timmy. He was glad to see them go. "Let's go."

"Yeah, go ahead," urged Bobbie. "See you back here."

Although he was still suspicious of his two partners, Ray drove off.

Carl frowned. "I wanted some ice cream," he said wistfully.

Bobbie shoved him toward the apartment building steps. *"C'mon!"* he growled.

In the car, Ray had a troubled look on his face. "All of a sudden they're not sticking to us like ticks anymore," he thought aloud. "Like they trust me. Did you tell him anything?"

Timmy shrugged. "Only that they shouldn't worry about me telling you where the hiding place is," he answered. "I promised I'd do it when we were all together."

"And they *bought* that?"

"Guess so. Now they don't need to come with us anywhere."

Ray thought for a moment, then smiled. For the moment, he thought, it seemed he had the upper hand.

Back at the apartment, Bobbie and Carl ravaged the rooms as they searched for anything that might look like a map to the hidden money.

"Gotta be here somewhere," said Bobbie as he rifled through Timmy's suitcase. "Little weasel thinks he can outsmart me. . . . If he was my kid . . ."

"Hey," Carl called out from near the bed. "Look what I found."

He had hoisted the mattress and pulled out a folded square of paper. Bobbie grabbed the paper out of Carl's hands and opened it. On it was a maze of dotted lines all leading to a big X in the lower left-hand corner.

"This is it!" exclaimed Bobby happily. "This is it! X marks the spot where he hid all the coins. But it's all in some kind of code."

In fact, there were symbols on the page that Bobbie could not understand.

"Can you figure it out?" asked Carl.

" 'Course I can," answered Bobbie. "He's a stupid kid, you think he can outsmart me?"

"He *is* in the ninety-fifth percentile, Bob," Carl reminded his partner.

"What's that supposed to mean?"

"I think it means he can outsmart you."

"Shut up," ordered Bobbie. He folded the map. "I got that little punk's number now. When he's with Ray tomorrow *we* go on a treasure hunt."

"What about Ray?" asked Carl.

"Look," explained Bobbie. "We find the coins, Ray gets his cut like everyone else. But if we tell him we got this map, he'll wanna come along and the kid could get suspicious, maybe switch hiding places. So we *keep* this to ourselves, all right?"

Carl nodded. It made perfect sense to him.

"But we can't take the original," Bobbie continued. "Kid would know we found it. I gotta make a copy."

"Drugstore on the corner's got a copy machine," said Carl.

Bobbie shot out the door.

"Hey," Carl called after him "Bring back some ice cream!"

But Bobbie, already halfway down the stairs, didn't hear Carl. His thoughts were planning ahead to tomorrow. By then he would have his own copy of the treasure map. Then he and Carl would find the hidden coins, bring them to Dobbs, and get all the money for themselves. It would be a clean two-way split.

And Ray Gleason, he smiled greedily, would never see a penny of it.

15.
Just Like
a Real Dad

Detectives Theresa Walsh and Alex Ceranski parked their car across the street from the Baskin-Robbins ice cream parlor and waited. A light rain was beginning to fall and they were getting tired. They had been following Ray Gleason for the last two days and there was still no sign of illegal activity. Now, as they waited for Ray and Timmy to come out of the ice cream parlor, they wondered when they would see some sign of "Dobbs."

"So why're they taking the boy everywhere they go?" asked Theresa.

"Maybe he's the brains of the outfit," joked Ceranski.

"Or maybe he's got something on them," Theresa said, thinking out loud. Although it was an unlikely explanation, it was the only reason she could think of. "Let's take separate cars tomorrow in case they split up again," she suggested. She remembered that the other two suspects, Bobbie

80

and Carl, were not with Ray and Timmy in the ice cream parlor.

"Ceranski, we've got the handoff," a filtered voice crackled over their car radio. It was Detective Zinn. Theresa and Ceranski looked behind them and saw Zinn and another officer pull up in an unmarked police car. It was their relief.

"So, you want to go somewhere?" Ceranski asked Theresa. They were both off duty now.

But Theresa's eyes were fixed on Timmy. She could see him through the window of the ice cream parlor. He was sitting across from his father, working on a rather large hot-fudge sundae.

"I'm busy," she answered.

"I wasn't asking you for a date," Ceranski retorted. "I said — "

"I know what you said," Theresa said, cutting her partner off. "And I said I'm busy."

Ceranski dropped the subject. Getting to the human side of his partner seemed impossible. He was beginning to wonder if she even *had* a human side.

Inside the ice cream parlor, Ray tapped his fingers against his coffee cup as he watched Timmy take another bite of his ice cream.

"So, Tim," he began. "You've had a pretty good time these last few days, haven't you? You can't say I haven't kept up my end of the deal. You can't say that. So, I was thinking. Maybe we can go get the coins tonight. Get that out of the way, clear the decks, so we don't have to worry about it anymore."

Timmy mulled the idea over. Then he shook his head.

"That's not our deal, Dad," he replied. "Our deal is for the week. But what if we do this, Dad: What if we gave the coins back?"

"Gave the coins back?" Ray asked, stunned.

"You see, Dad, I've been thinking," Timmy explained. "If I tell you where the coins are, you're going to get caught."

"What're you talking about?"

"You *always* get caught, Dad. You're not a good thief. I mean, get real."

Ray's face turned red. "Look," he said. "Don't you worry about me getting caught. I got this planned, okay? I mean I did until *you* showed up."

Timmy looked down at his sundae. A hurt expression came over his face.

"I'm tired of lying to my friends," he said without looking at his father. " 'Where's your dad? How come he never comes to see you?' 'Oh, he's in the CIA, he's on a secret mission somewhere.' I couldn't tell them where you *really* were. It's embarrassing."

"Oh, I embarrass you?" asked Ray. "Well, how about when I own my own bakery? Is that going to embarrass you?"

"I'll always know how you got it," Timmy answered flatly. "Whoever gets the coins is going to get caught. I don't want it to be you."

"Now listen, Tim," Ray said in an insistent voice. "We got a deal here. I give you what you want, then you give me what I want. Are we clear on that?"

Timmy looked at his father for a long moment. His hurt expression turned to one of disappointment.

"You'll never change," he said.

"I'm *trying* to, if you'd just cooperate."

Timmy stood up. "Well, maybe I won't," he said defiantly.

"Sit down, Tim."

But Timmy grabbed his backpack and ran out of the ice cream parlor.

"*Tim!*" Ray ran after him.

Outside the rain was falling more heavily. Timmy ran down the street and around the corner. By the time Ray emerged from the ice cream parlor, Timmy was nowhere to be seen. Ray quickly raced to his car, climbed in, and drove off to search for his son.

A few blocks away Timmy turned down a dark side street. Unable to see where he was going through the pouring rain, he bumped hard into a couple of tough-looking men. Both wore leather jackets and were unshaven. They looked greedily at his backpack.

"Whoa," said one of the tough guys, "where you running to, boy?"

Timmy was nervous. He tried to sidestep the men, but they stepped in front of him and blocked his path.

"What'cha got in that pack there?" asked the second man.

"Nothing," said Timmy. "I have to get home."

The second man grabbed the backpack, but Timmy held on to it. The two men laughed as they tried to wriggle the backpack free.

"Oooh, he's a fighter, ain't he?" joked one of the men.

"It's mine!" yelled Timmy, unwilling to let go of the pack.

"Leave him alone!" a voice from behind commanded them. Timmy and the two toughs turned to see Ray standing there, rain bouncing off of him. "Go on," he ordered. "Clear out of here!"

Without warning, one of the backpack robbers brought his leg up into Ray's stomach. Ray doubled over in pain. The two thieves broke out into laughter.

Then Ray leaped onto the thieves. He nailed one of them with a thunderous punch across the jaw and hit the other with a short, powerful stomach-to-chin combination. Both crooks went down to the pavement with a thud.

Ray then picked up a nearby trash can and lifted it over his head. But before he could bring it down on their heads, both street punks scrambled to their feet and ran off.

Ray slowly put the trash can down. He was breathing heavily, hurting from the kick to his stomach.

Timmy stared at his father, almost speechless at his heroics.

"Are you all right?" Timmy asked.

"Get in the car," said Ray, wincing in pain.

Timmy wasn't sure what to do. "I'm sorry," he began. "I — "

"Get — in — the — car!"

Timmy quickly obeyed and climbed into Ray's car, which was parked at the curb. A few seconds later Ray climbed into the driver's side. Both of them just sat there for several long, uncertain moments.

Timmy looked at his father. Ray had just saved his life. Did that mean that Ray cared about him the way a dad should care about his son? Timmy wondered. Ray was sure starting to *act* like a real dad.

"So what're we doing tomorrow, Dad?" Timmy asked.

Ray threw Timmy a dour look. But then the look gave way to a grin, the grin to a wry snort of laughter.

Just like a real dad, Timmy thought as he smiled back at Ray.

And he was starting to feel just like a real son, too.

16.
Theresa Gets
Some Advice

O'Reilly's Bar N' Grill never seemed to close. That was because it was only two blocks away from the precinct and always filled with off-duty police officers who had just finished their shifts.

Theresa didn't normally hang out at O'Reilly's. When her shifts were finished she'd usually go straight home, make herself a TV dinner, and dig into one of the many police procedural manuals she enjoyed studying.

But the rain was still coming down hard by the time she and Ceranski returned to the precinct after handing over the surveillance of Ray Gleason to their replacements. She decided to take her study manual to O'Reilly's, have a drink, and wait until the rain cleared.

But the local police hangout was not a place to find privacy. And it was too noisy to study. No sooner had she ordered a soda than she glanced up and saw Ceranski, who had just entered the restaurant.

Now he was heading straight toward her.

Theresa quickly opened her police procedural manual and pretended to look like she was absorbed in her studies.

"Thought you were busy," Ceranski said as he approached her.

"I am," said Theresa, without looking up from the book.

Ceranski took the book from her and looked at the cover. *Crime Scene Procedures*," he read aloud. "I read this once. I won't tell you how it ends."

Theresa took her book back and resumed reading.

"You know, Walsh," Ceranski continued. "You gotta learn to relax, let your hair down. Just 'cause your dad was the greatest cop in the solar system doesn't mean you gotta be just like him twenty-four hours a day."

Theresa ignored the remark. Ceranski picked up her drink and sniffed it.

"7Up," he recognized the smell. "How 'bout I buy you a real drink?"

"No thanks."

"Hey, I'm just trying to break the ice here," said Ceranski. "What's going on? What'd I do to you, huh?"

Theresa finally looked up at her partner. "Just stop treating me like — like I don't know what I'm doing," she finally blurted out. "I can do the job, Ceranski. I can *do* it."

"Lieutenant Romayko's the one to convince, not me," Ceranski responded. "But I could give you some help."

Theresa turned back to her book and tried to ignore Ceranski.

"When you're working surveillance," Ceranski said, "how 'bout trying to fit in, dress like other attractive women your age, not like a cop? And for Pete's sake, get rid of those shoes."

On those words, Ceranski abruptly turned and walked away. For a few moments Theresa continued to act as if she hadn't been listening to her partner. But after he'd gone, she glanced down at her feet and frowned at her familiar clunky sensible shoes.

She thought Ceranski might be right.

17.
Like Father,
Like Son

"Where's my toothbrush?" asked Ray as he rummaged through his bathroom medicine cabinet the next morning.

Timmy stuck his head in the door. "I threw it out," he told his father.

"You threw it out?"

"The bristles were all matted and stuff," explained Timmy. "You're supposed to change your toothbrush every three months. Didn't you know that?"

Then Timmy walked over to the toothbrush holder where two new toothbrushes were hanging. He handed one to Ray.

Later, on the way to the park to play basketball, Ray decided he didn't like the idea of Timmy telling him when to buy a new toothbrush.

"A toothbrush is a personal thing," he said as he and Timmy dribbled the ball back and forth between each other. "And *I'll* decide when mine's expired."

"But the bristles were matted," insisted Timmy.

"I don't care if the bristles were matted," said Ray. "I *like* matted bristles."

"Well maybe we can run over your new toothbrush with the car," joked Timmy. "Would that make you happy?"

"It might," answered Ray. Then he laughed. "Very funny."

Across the street Theresa Walsh watched as Ray and Timmy continued on their way. But today she looked different. Instead of her usual flat, sensible shoes, she now wore a sportier pair with a narrow toe and heels. And instead of her conservative gray dress suit, she now wore a slightly shorter pleated skirt and cardigan sweater.

She even had some makeup on her face. .

Ceranski had been right, she realized. Dressed this way, she blended in better with the civilians. No one would suspect she was a cop.

On the way to the park Ray stopped in front of a bakery. There was a big wedding cake in the window.

"Now look at that," said Ray.

Timmy looked at the cake. It looked all right to him. "It's a cake," he said.

"Look at that crummy detail work on that frosting," Ray commented. "People who ruin baked goods like that should get arrested."

Timmy didn't notice the frosting at first, but after Ray pointed it out to him he agreed that it was, indeed, crummy.

As soon as they reached the park, they raced each other to a basketball court. Timmy got there first, with Ray lagging far behind. He knew his father had let him win the race. Then they began shooting baskets one-on-one. Ray sunk one in from the center line.

"Whoa, not bad!" exclaimed Timmy.

"Not bad?" frowned Ray. "I was second-team all-conference in high school."

"I didn't know that," said Timmy. He was impressed.

"A lotta things you don't know, kid." Ray dribbled around Timmy. Timmy had a hard time staying with the ball. "Like how to guard someone," commented Ray. "Get your hands up, get on the balls of your feet."

Timmy followed the instructions, raising his hands, guarding his father.

"How come you didn't go to college?" asked Timmy breathlessly.

"Because I had to get a job first," answered Ray as he darted around the court. "I was working a loading dock for eighty-nine-fifty a week, trying to save for college. Guy comes to me and says, 'Wanna earn five hundred bucks? Look the other way when our trucks back up!' "

Ray sunk another basket.

"I'm not making excuses," he added. "I needed the money and I took a shortcut."

"Just like you're doing now," said Timmy. Ray knew he was referring to the coin robbery.

"Yeah," admitted Ray. "But this is the last time."

Just then, two attractive-looking women in jogging clothes ran by the court. Ray dribbled the ball beside them.

"Ladies," he said. "How 'bout a little basketball game here? Hey, it's a great calorie burner. Tim-boy, tell 'em."

The women jogged off, ignoring Ray. Ray just laughed. Then he threw Timmy a look of mock disappointment.

"Nice going," he said to Timmy. "Some clever patter on your part, we coulda gotten dates with those two."

Timmy shrugged. "What was I supposed to say?" he said. The idea made him uncomfortable.

Ray stopped bouncing the basketball. "Don't you know how to talk to girls? I can't believe you're my son."

"It's not something I like to brag about," Timmy answered red-faced.

"Okay," said Ray, taking on the tone of a teacher. "How to pick up girls: First, get 'em talking. Now pretend I'm some fabulous babe you want to hit on."

Ray suddenly put his hand on his hip and began strutting around, pretending to be a girl.

"*Dad,*" Timmy groaned.

"C'mon," insisted Ray. "Gimme a line, stranger. C'mon, handsome, I'm getting away here, I'm walking outta your life — "

Timmy groped for something to say. "Um . . . um . . . nice basketball!" he blurted out.

Ray batted his eyelashes at Timmy. "Oh? You think so?" he said in a soft, feminine voice.

"Um . . . yeah," Timmy played along. "Where'd you get it?"

"Perfect! Perfect!" Ray exclaimed in his own voice. "Disarm 'em with a compliment, follow with a question. Now you got the lady's attention. You say: 'So, I notice you got the Michael Jordan autographed ball there.' And she says: 'Oh, yes. Michael is my favorite player.' And you say: 'Me, too. Say, if you've got a few minutes, would you like to go for coffee?' And she says: 'Oh, I never thought you'd ask.' See? It's that easy."

"It is?"

"Give it a shot," said Ray. And with that he aimed a thirty-footer straight into the basket.

While Ray and Timmy spent the morning playing in the park together, Bobbie and Carl spent the morning on a treasure hunt. They stood in the center of town under a large American flag, with

Timmy's treasure map unfolded before them. They were trying to figure out which direction to go.

A few feet away, in his unmarked police car, Ceranski followed them.

"Look," said Bobbie, pointing to the flag. "The map starts at a picture of a flag, right? That's gotta mean *this* flag. We start *here*."

"What makes you so sure it's this flag?" asked Carl.

" 'Cause it's a big flag, it's near Ray's place. It's gotta be this one," insisted Bobbie. "Okay. The map says go east for seventy-five giant steps. Go ahead. Count 'em off."

Carl faced east and then moved off with very large giant steps. Bobbie chased after him.

"Hey, whattaya doing?" groaned Bobbie. "Those are *your* giant steps. It's gotta be *kid* giant steps."

"Oh," said Carl, coming to a stop. "So how big are kid giant steps?"

That was a good question, thought Bobbie. He stopped a kid about Timmy's age who was crossing the street with his mother and their Doberman.

"Hey, lady," Bobbie asked the boy's mother. "Let us use your kid for a minute."

The boy's mother, thinking they were being accosted by a maniac, yanked her son away from Bobbie. She sicked her Doberman at the two strangers. Bobbie and Carl leaped back, fearful of the dog's snapping, vicious teeth.

"Okay, okay, forget it!" exclaimed Bobbie in a pleading tone. The woman pulled back the dog and walked away with her son. Bobbie turned to Carl. "Ask for a little help these days," he began, "you get your head bit off. Where were we?"

"Giant steps," said Carl.

"Yeah, yeah," Bobbie remembered. "Okay, let's say one of your giant steps equals two of the kid's. So half of seventy-five is thirty-seven-and-a-half. Take thirty-seven-and-a-half giant steps that way."

Carl faced east again and resumed walking.

After their basketball game, Ray left Timmy on a street corner and slipped into a phone booth.

"Dobbs," Ray said after placing his call. An answering machine had picked up on the other end. "It's Ray. I guess you're out. I just wanted to leave you this message. We're set for Sunday. I got the merchandise. No problem."

Outside the phone booth Timmy bounced the basketball and waited for his dad. The ball hit his foot and then bounced out into the street.

Timmy ran after the ball. He didn't see that he was in the path of an oncoming bus.

"LOOK OUT!" someone shouted at Timmy. Timmy froze. The bus whizzed by him. The basketball bounced across to the opposite side of the street.

The basketball stopped at the feet of the woman who had shouted out to him. Timmy looked over at her. She was beautiful.

It was Theresa.

"Can I have my ball, please?" Timmy asked.

"Stay *right* there!" Theresa commanded. She picked up the ball and crossed over to Timmy. "Don't you know not to dart into traffic like that?" she reprimanded him. "You *never* run into the street without looking both ways!"

Timmy was taken aback. "Gee — okay," he muttered. "I'm sorry."

Just then Ray stepped out of the phone booth and marched over to Timmy's defense.

"Hey, what's going on here?" he demanded to know.

"He ran into the street and was almost hit by a bus," Theresa replied angrily. "*That's* what's going on."

Ray swatted Timmy harmlessly across the head. "What's wrong with you?" he asked. Then he turned apologetically to Theresa. "He's got a habit of running off. Good you were watching him. Thanks."

Theresa looked at Ray for a moment. He was a much more handsome man when she could look into his eyes. Then she remembered that she was a cop. She couldn't let on that she had been tailing them.

"I wasn't watching," she said. "I was just crossing the street and, well . . ." She handed the ball back to Timmy. "Just look both ways next time."

With that, Theresa turned and started away.

"Nice sweater," Timmy called after her. "Where'd you get it?"

Theresa stopped. "Sears," she said. She was startled that Timmy would ask. "I got it at Sears."

Timmy smiled. "You wanna go for coffee?" he asked just like his father had taught him.

Theresa let out a half smile. She was speechless.

Timmy glanced up at his father expecting to hear some smart-aleck remark.

But for the first time that day Ray was speechless, too.

18.
A Surprise Guest

They sat at a table in a coffee shop. Ray and Theresa were sipping coffee. Timmy was having milk and a chocolate-frosted donut.

"So what do you do, Theresa?" Ray asked.

Theresa hesitated. "I'm a teacher," she finally said. "I, uh, teach kindergarten."

"That's gotta be a tough job," said Ray. "You must like kids."

"Oh, yes," said Theresa. She didn't have to lie about it, either. "Children are special."

Just then Timmy put two straws in his nose and blew into his glass of milk. When he looked up and saw Ray and Theresa staring at him, he stopped.

"What line of work are you in?" Theresa asked Ray.

"He makes cakes." Timmy jumped in. "And decorates them."

"Oh, that's quite an art," said Theresa. "I took a class in that once."

"So did he," said Timmy. "When he was in —
uh — *college*."

Ray looked at Theresa. "Folsom U.," he said
honestly. "It's a state institution."

"Oh," Theresa said. "You mean the prison."

Ray nodded. Theresa was impressed with his
honesty. She found herself wishing she could be
as honest with him. Somehow, here in the coffee
shop, Ray did not seem like the criminal type.
Especially when she looked at Timmy and the
chocolate mustache that now surrounded his lips.

"He didn't shoot anybody or anything," said
Timmy coming to Ray's defense. "He just stole
something and — right, Dad?"

"Yeah, I stole something," admitted Ray. "But
that was a long time ago. And you could say I'm
a different man now."

Ray threw Theresa a disarming smile. She wondered: Could she be wrong about him?

"We're going to the museum this afternoon,"
said Timmy. "Want to come with us?"

Theresa hesitated. It was against police pro-
cedure to go undercover without Lieutenant Romayko's approval.

"If you don't have anything else planned," Ray
urged.

"Well, yeah, I don't know," Theresa fumbled.
"I did have this thing. I was, um, going to meet
my dentist for, um, I have a tooth that's, um, but
it's feeling, um, better, the tooth, so let me see if

I can call and reschedule the appointment."

Theresa excused herself from the table to look for a pay phone.

"She's nice," Timmy said to Ray when Theresa had gone. "Do you like her?"

"Maybe," answered Ray.

Ray thought for a moment. He did like her, but something about her made him nervous.

Theresa found the pay phone in the back of the coffee shop, but she didn't call her dentist. She called Ceranski. Ceranski didn't like the idea of her going undercover. Not only was it unauthorized, but it wasn't safe.

But Theresa insisted. She had already gotten Ray and Timmy's confidence. It was too late to back out now.

Theresa hung up and returned to the table. Ray paid for the food and the three of them took a trolley car to the Museum of Modern Art.

The first thing they saw was a large black-and-white abstract painting. Strange shapes and lines were strewn across the canvas. Timmy twisted his head upside down trying to make some sense of it.

"I don't get it," he said.

"It's called abstract expressionism," explained Theresa. "This artist is known for his bold brush-work. His use of positive and negative space."

Timmy looked askance at Theresa. Her explanation was more confusing than the painting itself.

"Timmy," said Ray, pointing to the painting. "Tell me what you see here."

"Paint," said Timmy. "A buncha paint."

"Exactly," said Ray. "You see, this artist *wants* you to see the brush strokes. It's not some three-dimensional illusion like those other paintings we saw. It's just a *buncha* paint, Tim. That's it."

Timmy's eyes brightened. "Ohhh," he said with understanding. "Cool."

Theresa smiled. It was the second time that day she had been impressed with Ray.

Ray stood Timmy in front of another painting. To Timmy it looked like a million colored dots. Then Ray told Timmy to close his eyes and guided him a few feet back. When Timmy opened his eyes the same painting now looked like a bunch of people spending the day in a park.

"Millions of little dots, Tim," explained Ray. "Up close they don't look like much, but put 'em all together. Sometimes at first glance things aren't what they seem."

Ray turned to Theresa. "I guess that goes for people, too, huh?" he asked her.

"Does it?" replied Theresa. She wasn't sure if he was talking about her or himself.

"Like you take cops," continued Ray. "They think they have this special ability to look at you and know who you are. Once a con, always a con.

But lots of times they're wrong. That's the one thing I don't like about cops. They assume too much."

Theresa paused. Was he on to her, she wondered?

"I assure you," she said carefully. "I don't make a habit of assuming."

"Neither do I," nodded Ray.

Later, after looking at all the exhibits in the museum, Timmy wanted to go to the gift shop. Ray browsed through some books. Theresa pretended to look through some posters. After a moment she realized that Timmy had been standing next to her for some time. He was smiling.

"You smell like my mother," he told her. "Your perfume. What is it?"

"It's White Linen."

"She used to wear that a lot."

"Does she live in San Francisco?"

"She's dead," answered Timmy grimly. "She had cancer."

"Oh." Theresa gently sighed. "I'm sorry."

"It was three years ago," explained Timmy. "I live with my aunt in Redding now. She's nice, but she married this real dork. He doesn't even want me around. So I think I'm going to move in with my dad. You know, permanently. He needs me."

Timmy walked off and joined Ray at the bookshelf. Theresa stared after him. At that moment,

Timmy seemed very fragile to her. She wondered what would become of him if she got the evidence that would put his father in jail again.

For the first time since she had started this assignment, she hoped she was wrong about Ray.

19.
X Marks the Spot

It took Carl 679 baby steps to come to the end of Timmy's map. When he was finished, he and Bobbie found themselves standing in an alley behind a restaurant. At the far end of the alley was a trash Dumpster. On the wall above the Dumpster was a faded red *X*.

"There!" pointed Bobbie. "An *X*. *X* marks the spot!"

"You think he hid it in here?" asked Carl as they approached the Dumpster. "Seems kinda dumb. Trash truck could come along, haul it away."

"So maybe the kid ain't so smart after all," said Bobbie.

Bobbie opened the Dumpster lid. He and Carl held their noses and peeked inside. All they could see were flies buzzing over piles of rotted vegetables and food scraps.

"Get in and take a look," said Bobbie as he winced at the smell.

"I'm not getting in there," said Carl. He was wearing one of his most expensive Pierre Cardin suits.

"A fortune at our fingertips and you're worried about your suit," Bobbie accused his partner.

"You buy your clothes at a garage sale," Carl retorted. "*You* go in there."

Bobbie sighed hopelessly. Then he squeezed his nose tight and climbed into the Dumpster.

"Go keep a lookout," he ordered Carl.

Carl strolled back to the alley entrance. Across the street was a pushcart vendor selling hot pretzels. Carl crossed over and bought one smothered in mustard. He began munching it hungrily.

Meanwhile, a busboy emerged from the restaurant next to the alley and emptied a bag full of trash into the Dumpster. Then he closed the lid hard on Bobbie's head.

Bobbie tried to push the lid open from inside, but the knock to his head made him very groggy. Soon he heard the sound of a truck motor approaching outside the Dumpster. Suddenly Bobbie felt the Dumpster being lifted from the ground. He pushed the lid open and saw that he was being emptied into a garbage truck.

Carl could hear Bobbie's screams from all the way across the street. He dropped his pretzel and raced back to the alley just in time to pull Bobbie out of the Dumpster before the trash was crushed by the garbage truck's compactor.

The garbage men looked quizzically at Bobbie and Carl as the two men apologized, excused themselves, and left the alley.

Once back out on the street, Bobbie opened the map again. He realized that they must have taken a wrong turn somewhere so he and Carl retraced their steps. When they were done they found themselves standing in front of an old church.

Now they were more confused than ever. They couldn't find an X anywhere. Then Bobbie looked up at the church spire. On top of it sat a cross.

"It's not an X," Bobbie realized. "It's a *cross.*" Then he held up the map, turned it sideways and looked at it again. He was right. The X *could* be a cross.

Bobbie and Carl went inside the church. It was a cavernous place with vaulted ceilings, an ornately decorated altar, stained-glass windows, and statues of the apostles along both walls.

The church was empty, except for them. Bobbie lit a cigarette.

"This place is like a 7-Eleven," he said. "It's open all night. It's a perfect place for him to hide the coins."

"Hey," said Carl. He pointed to Bobbie's cigarette. "God don't allow smoking."

Bobbie rolled his eyes and started to put his cigarette out in a font of holy water, but Carl grabbed his wrist and jerked it away. Bobbie then dropped the cigarette to the ground and stamped it out with his foot.

Then they began to look for the coins.

Carl looked behind the organ pit. Bobbie looked behind the flickering votive candles. There he saw a small box. He knew it was a donation box. He also knew it was the best place a kid might think of to hide a bunch of coins.

But as Bobbie reached into the donation box, Carl slipped and leaned haphazardly against the organ keys. A loud musical blast filled the church.

From inside the sacristy room behind the altar, a nun heard the organ blast. Peeking out, she saw Bobbie reaching his hand into the donation box. He didn't find the coins there, but was stuffing what money he could into his pockets.

She quickly went to her phone and dialed 911.

Meanwhile, Bobbie joined Carl at the communion rail. Before them hung the figure of Christ on the cross. They looked at the figure. It seemed to be watching them with accusing eyes.

Bobbie motioned for Carl to go up to the sanctuary and take a look around. Carl refused to go. Bobbie pushed him, but Carl refused and shoved Bobbie back. Finally, Bobbie climbed over the rail and crouched behind the satin drapery that adorned the sanctuary. Behind it he saw a sealed cardboard box. He grabbed the box and pulled it out from behind the drapes.

As he and Carl turned to leave, the nun emerged from the sacristy.

"Stop! Thieves!" she shouted at them.

Bobbie and Carl bolted over the communion rail and through the rows of wooden pews. The nun grabbed a candlestick and chased after them. They dodged her blows until they were able to dash out the front doors of the church.

But once outside they came to a crashing stop. Two police cars were parked on the sidewalk and several officers were standing on the steps of the church. Their guns were drawn.

"Don't move!" ordered one of the officers. "Hands up over your heads!"

Bobbie and Carl's hands shot up over their heads and they froze. The box Bobbie had stolen slipped out of his hands and fell to the ground. It smashed open. Bobbie glanced down expecting to see the hidden coins spread out over the steps.

But instead of coins, a collection of wine bottles rolled out of the box and down the steps.

Timmy had outsmarted them yet again.

20.
A Wish for Timmy

Theresa and Timmy walked alone along the docks at Aquatic Park. The sun was reflecting brightly off the water and they could see sea gulls silhouetted along the rails of the wharf.

"So you're a teacher, huh?" asked Timmy. "My teacher, Mrs. Carver, she's fat. She's not like you." Timmy paused. "I think my dad likes you, too," he blurted out after a minute.

"Well, I like the both of you," Theresa replied.

"Can I ask you a question?" Timmy asked politely.

"Sure."

"If you had a secret that someone really wanted to know, but you knew if you told them it'd get them in big trouble, would you tell them the secret anyway?"

Theresa thought about what Timmy had asked. She wondered if he wasn't trying to tell her something.

"I don't know," answered Theresa. "Maybe you

could tell me what the secret is and I could tell you what I'd do."

But just as Timmy opened his mouth to answer, Ray returned from the snack stand with bags of popcorn.

"Here's the popcorn," he said, handing Timmy and Theresa a bag each.

"Thanks," said Theresa.

Now all three continued to walk along the wharf. As they walked, Ray gently nudged Timmy out of earshot of Theresa.

"What's between us is between *us*, all right?" he reminded Timmy gently.

Timmy nodded. "Sure, Dad." Then he ran off and scattered some popcorn to the sea gulls.

Later Ray thought it might be time for dinner. But Timmy wanted to make one more stop first. He told Ray to take him to the Neiman Marcus department store. Once there, Timmy took some money from his father and then disappeared into the crowd of shoppers.

"He says he lives with his aunt," Theresa commented to Ray once Timmy was out of earshot.

"My sister," explained Ray. "She's got a nice big house there in Redding. There's good schools. He's got all his friends. He's better off there."

"He doesn't think so," said Theresa. "He told me he'd rather live with you."

Ray paused. "He said that?"

Suddenly Timmy came running up to them. He pulled a small box out of a shopping bag and handed it to Theresa.

"For you," he said. "Open it."

Theresa took the box. "For me? Why?"

"I could've been roadkill today," he reminded her. "You saved me. Open it."

Theresa fumbled with the ribbon and opened the box. It was a bottle of White Linen perfume. Her favorite.

"It's White Linen," Timmy told Ray. "She likes the stuff Mom used to wear."

"I noticed," said Ray. Theresa's perfume had reminded him of his late wife right from the start.

"You can wear it tonight when we go to dinner," Timmy told Theresa.

"Next thing he'll be proposing," joked Ray. He and Theresa laughed. "Are you free?"

Theresa hesitated. Against her better judgment she was getting involved with Ray and Timmy. But one look at Timmy and she knew she had to go to dinner with them.

On the way out of the store they passed a mannequin dressed for outdoor sports. Around the dummy's shoulder was a blue sports bag identical to the one Ray used to carry the stolen coins in.

"Hey, Dad," called Timmy. "That looks just like — "

"Yeah, yeah," interrupted Ray as he pulled

Timmy away from the mannequin. "The bag I keep my gym stuff in. Kids remember the dumbest things."

Ray smiled nervously at Theresa. Then he pushed Timmy forward and through the exit of the department store.

Theresa went home and changed her clothes while she waited for Ray and Timmy to pick her up for dinner. She put on one of her prettiest dresses and brushed her hair loose. Then she spritzed herself with some of the White Linen perfume that Timmy had given her.

She was looking forward to spending the evening with Ray and Timmy.

Then her eyes fell on her gun, which was hanging holstered on a chair. Her face clouded. She remembered she was trying to nail Ray, not date him.

A short time later she was sitting opposite Ray and Timmy around a table in a small Italian restaurant. Timmy had picked the place. It was intimate and dimly lit. Romantic music was playing in the background.

"I like your hair that way," Ray told Theresa after they had finished the main course. A waiter was removing the dishes. "Looks pretty."

"Thank you," replied Theresa. Then, remembering what her job was, she took on a more serious tone. "So, Ray," she began, "you like where you're working? You plan to stay there?"

"Yeah, I plan to stay there," Ray answered. "In fact, I may even buy the place."

"That's great," said Theresa. She had to admit to herself that she was impressed yet again. Still, she had to wonder where Ray could get the money to buy a bakery. "If you don't mind my asking," she continued, "How do you get financing for that? Do you get a small business loan?"

"Yeah, a loan," Ray lied. "I'm kinda waiting for that to come through."

Ray and Timmy exchanged knowing glances. They knew exactly where the money for the bakery was coming from — and it wasn't a loan.

"The Dodgers are coming in next week, Dad," Timmy said, changing the subject. "You think we could go?"

Ray knew that Timmy was really asking if he could stay with him longer. But Ray also knew that was impossible.

Just then they were interrupted by the sound of the waiters singing "Happy Birthday." The waiters brought a candlelit cake to the table. Across the top of the cake was written: HAPPY BIRTHDAY TIMMY.

Timmy was really surprised and very confused. He looked at Ray. It wasn't his birthday.

"Just say it's for all the birthdays I missed, Tim," explained Ray. "Sorry I couldn't make the cake myself."

For once, Timmy was speechless.

"Well, c'mon," Ray urged. "Make a wish and blow out the candles before the fire sprinklers come on."

Timmy happily closed his eyes and made a wish. After he blew out all the candles he opened his eyes. He wanted to tell Ray what he had wished for, but he knew if he did, it wouldn't come true.

He had wished he could stay with his dad and Theresa forever.

After dinner Ray, Timmy, and Theresa went for a walk. It was a warm night and many couples were out taking strolls. Some even had their children with them. Timmy bought a package of sparklers and began tracing designs with them in the air.

"So why'd you become a teacher?" Ray asked Theresa.

"My dad was a teacher," Theresa lied. "I never wanted to be anything else."

"That's good," said Ray. "You knew what you wanted and you went for it. I wasn't sure what I wanted. So I became a thief."

Theresa paused. "But you're not a thief anymore," she said.

"Yeah, right," said Ray looking away from her. " 'Course I told the same thing to my ex-wife when we got married. And then when Timmy was five I got arrested again and went to jail. She never forgave me for that. Said if I didn't love them enough to stay out of jail, then I didn't love them enough. And the best thing I could do was just get out of their lives. Don't write, don't call. Just be dead, you know? So I was."

"I guess you have to decide what you want," said Theresa. "What's most important."

For a moment they both looked over at Timmy. He seemed caught up in the designs he was making with his sparklers. Then they looked at each other. Their eyes met. Ray leaned over and kissed Theresa on the lips. Theresa knew she should back away, but didn't. She gently kissed him back.

After a minute Theresa broke away. Ray could sense that something was wrong.

"Was that wrong?" Ray asked apologetically.

"No," said Theresa with uncertainty. "But it's late and I have to get home. Thanks for dinner and, um, everything."

"Well, I hope I see you again," Ray said softly. He meant it, too.

"Good-bye," said Theresa. And with that she turned and disappeared into the night.

Theresa had just left the park when her partner, Ceranski approached.

"What are you doing here?" she demanded.

"I could ask you the same question," replied Ceranski.

"I'm just doing my job — "

"Oh, really," Ceranski said with a smirk. "Well,

they must be teaching some new stuff at the academy, 'cause I don't think we were allowed to kiss the suspect."

Theresa realized Ceranski had been watching her the whole time. She searched her mind for an explanation, but found none. Ceranski was right. What she was doing was completely against the rules.

21.
The Truth
About Theresa

"Who gave you the authority to start going steady with the suspect?" Lieutenant Romayko angrily led Theresa toward his precinct office as he reprimanded her.

"Sir, I'm sorry," replied Theresa. "I know I got too close, but I think it's going to pay off. The suspect's son told me he knows something that his father wants him to tell him, but the boy is afraid to tell him because that could mean the father could get in trouble."

Romayko cocked his eyebrow at the fantastic explanation. "Do you just make this stuff up, Walsh?" he asked sarcastically. "Or do you have it written down someplace?"

Theresa unfolded a slip of paper and showed it to Romayko. It was the treasure map found on Bobbie and Carl when they were arrested at the church.

"The two arrested at the church had this," explained Theresa. "They're not talking, but I think it's a treasure map, sir. I think the boy drew it. I think he knows where the coins are."

"In that case that kid's an accessory to the crime," said Romayko as they reached his office. "And we don't let him out of our sight."

Theresa furrowed her brow. What Lieutenant Romayko said was true. Withholding evidence made Timmy as guilty as his father. Now Timmy was a suspect, too.

The next morning, while Ray brushed his teeth with his new toothbrush, Timmy watched the videotape he had made of his week with his dad.

He watched everything, reliving every minute. There were the rides in the amusement park, the fish at the aquarium, and the game at the miniature golf course.

Finally, Timmy watched as his dad skated around the ice rink. He laughed loudly as he saw Ray collide with Bobbie and Carl. He played that part over and over again.

Then he paused the tape and moved in for a closer look. Something in the background of the scene caught his eye. Standing behind the glass around the rink's edge was Theresa — a full day before he met her while chasing after his basketball.

He wondered if her being at the ice rink was just a coincidence or something more.

Just then Ray entered the living room. Timmy

quickly turned off the videotape so his dad wouldn't see Theresa on the screen.

"Listen, Tim," said Ray as he buttoned his shirt. "I gotta go to work for a few hours. How 'bout you come with me? You can watch me work."

"That's okay, Dad," answered Timmy as he clutched his remote control. "I think I'll stay here."

"You sure?"

"Yeah. You go ahead. I'll be fine."

"Okay," said Ray. "I'll be back around one."

Ray grabbed his keys and went out the door. As it closed behind Ray, Timmy turned back to the TV and switched the tape on again. He freeze-framed the picture. The picture was a little fuzzy, but it was definitely Theresa at the ice-skating rink.

Timmy went to the window and looked out. He saw Ray emerge from the building, get into his car, and drive off. Then he saw another car parked across the street. A man got out of the car and looked directly up at Timmy's window. Then the car started up and took off after Ray. The man stayed behind. It was Detective Zinn.

They were being followed by the cops, Timmy realized.

Then he realized that Theresa must be a cop, too.

Timmy quickly formulated a plan in his mind. He had to get the police off his trail so that his father wouldn't get into trouble. And he had to do it fast.

The first thing he did was put on his baseball cap, windbreaker, and backpack. He bounded down the front steps of the apartment building and started up the sidewalk. Peeking back, he made sure that the man who had gotten out of the car was following him.

The chase was on.

Turning the corner, Timmy nimbly darted around the street vendors and passersby. A delivery truck was unloading some boxes. Timmy vaulted over them and crossed the street.

Detective Zinn dashed around the side of the truck just in time to see Timmy hop onto a cable car that was going in the opposite direction.

Zinn breathlessly chased after the cable car, but it was too fast. Looking for a shortcut, he ran into an alley between two buildings. He came out on the other side just as the cable car was turning the corner.

Timmy jumped off the cable car and ran across the street to the entrance of the underground train station. The cop followed close behind. Timmy slid down the stairway banister, zooming past the startled looks of climbing people. Then he bought a farecard, fed it into the turnstile, and went through.

Zinn lumbered behind, pushing past the crowd as he chased Timmy.

Timmy ran to the end of the platform and waited for the train. He was standing next to a light-haired boy who was about his own age. The boy was with his chattering mother. Zinn saw Timmy, but stayed further back along the platform. He wasn't about to let the boy out of his sight.

A few moments later a train pulled into the station. Timmy entered the car and took a seat. He made sure to sit right across from the light-haired boy and his mother.

Detective Zinn stepped into the next subway car just before its doors closed. He immediately walked to the end of the car and looked through the rear window. He saw Timmy sitting in the next car reading a book. The cop sighed. There was no way he could lose Timmy now. He turned away from the window and relaxed.

Minutes later the train pulled into the next station. Zinn looked back through the window to see if Timmy was still there. He smiled. The boy hadn't moved. The doors closed and the train started off again.

That's when Zinn glanced toward the station platform and felt his heart jump. Timmy was standing outside the train smiling and waving at him!

Zinn panicked. How could a kid be in two places at once?

Zinn slid open the rear door and marched toward the boy in the next car. As he got closer he realized that it wasn't Timmy at all. It was the light-haired kid who got on with his mother at the last station.

"Billy," Zinn heard the mother ask the boy. "Where'd you get that jacket?"

"A kid gave it to me," the cop heard the boy reply. "Cool, huh?"

Zinn was astonished. Timmy had given the boy his baseball cap and jacket.

And he had given Zinn the slip.

Now that he had shaken the cop, Timmy went to the Greyhound bus station. Once there, he found a row of pay lockers. Then he pulled his father's blue sports bag out of his backpack. The coins inside made it seem like it weighed a ton. Timmy put the bag inside the locker and closed the door. Then he dropped some money into the pay slot and removed the key.

He smiled. Everything was going according to plan.

22.
A Call from Dobbs

Ray was carefully icing a wedding cake in the kitchen of the bakery when Mr. Wankmueller approached him.

"How's that family emergency come out?" asked Mr. Wankmueller. "Everything okay?"

"Yeah, everything's fine, Mr. Wankmueller," said Ray. "It was my son. He kinda came to visit and I needed to spend some time with him."

"That's good, Ray," smiled Mr. Wankmueller.

"Yeah," agreed Ray as he continued his work. "And I've been doing some thinking. He might be moving here."

"That's nice, Ray," said Mr. Wankmueller. "I've been doing some thinking, too. If you want to buy the place, it's yours."

Ray grabbed Mr. Wankmueller's hand and pumped it.

"You mean it?" asked Ray. He was overjoyed. "That's terrific, Mr. Wankmueller. This is great! I can't tell you how much this means to me!"

Just then the phone rang. It was for Ray.

It was Dobbs.

Dobbs was back in town and he was ready to meet Ray the next day and exchange the stolen coins for cash. Ray didn't let Dobbs know that he didn't exactly have the coins in his possession — that would blow the deal. So he agreed to meet Dobbs as scheduled.

Now he *had* to get those coins from Timmy.

After work Ray raced home.

"Timmy!" he called. "Where are you?"

Timmy came out of the bedroom. He didn't look as if he had been out at all.

"Hi, Dad," he said, greeting his father. "How was work?"

"Where are the coins, Tim?" Ray asked with a tone of urgency. "I need to know right now."

"Dad," said Tim. "The police. What if the police know?"

Ray was beginning to turn red with anger. "Tim, I don't want to ask you again — !"

"You'd go for the coins anyway, wouldn't you?" asked Tim. "You'd try to outsmart them, but you'd get caught."

The two of them, father and son, stared at each other for a moment. Finally, Timmy nodded to the elephant fern in the corner. Ray went over to the fern and dug his hands into the soil.

He pulled out the pay locker key.

"It's in a locker at the bus station," Timmy said quietly.

"Thanks, Tim," Ray sighed with relief. "You came through for me."

"Sure," Timmy agreed flatly. "Well, I guess I should pack."

"Pack?"

"I'm going home."

"What do you mean you're going home?" asked Ray. "I thought you wanted to live here."

"I do," said Timmy. "But not if you get the coins."

"What're you saying? I gotta choose between you and the coins?"

Timmy thought for a second. "Well, yeah," he said. " 'Cause if you take the coins, you'll never see me again. You'll be in prison. And this time I won't write."

Timmy walked off into the bedroom with his head hung low. Ray followed. He saw that Timmy had his suitcase open across the bed and was starting to pack.

"You're really making me angry here, Tim," Ray told him. "You have no right to make me choose between you and two hundred fifty grand! It's the biggest break of my life and I'm not letting it get away from me!"

But Timmy ignored his father and continued to pack.

"Fine," Ray said at last. "You want to go, then go. I don't need you!"

And with that Ray stormed back into the living room, picked up the elephant fern plant and hurled it through the open window and out onto the street.

A few seconds later there was a knock at the door.

Ray angrily opened the door. It was Theresa.

"Hi," said Theresa nervously. She was taken aback by Ray's red face. "Uh, I saw a plant fly out your window."

"It was dead," said Ray.

"Oh," said Theresa as she walked in. "Um, I had a great time last night, Ray, and — "

But Ray walked away from her. She sensed that he was preoccupied with something else. Nevertheless, she had just come from Lieutenant Romayko's office. Her boss had decided that she should try to get Timmy away from his father and gain the boy's confidence. Perhaps she could then find out where Ray had hidden the stolen coins.

"Is Timmy here?" she asked gingerly.

"Yeah, he's here," answered Ray curtly.

"Well, it was nice of him to get me that perfume," said Theresa. "And I thought, if it's okay with you, I'd take him to the movies or something. Just the two of us."

Just then Timmy emerged from the bedroom, wearing his pack and carrying his suitcase.

"He can't go," said Ray. "I'm taking him to the bus station. He's going home."

Theresa shot a quick glance at Timmy's suitcase. She wondered if the coins might be inside.

"Oh, that's too bad," she said.

"Yeah," said Ray. "And we're kinda pressed for time." He took Timmy's suitcase and led the boy toward the door.

"Timmy," Theresa called out. "It was really fun being with you. I hope we can do it again."

"Sure," Timmy replied, throwing Theresa a cold stare. Theresa felt that Timmy had seen right through her masquerade.

And he had.

"Ray, wait — " said Theresa. "Isn't there any way I can get you to change your plans?"

"No," replied Ray. "I gotta go."

Theresa followed Ray and Timmy downstairs. She watched as the two of them got into Ray's car and drove off.

Then she got into her own car and followed them. As she did so she called headquarters and told them that Ray and Timmy were headed for the bus station and that the coins might be in Timmy's suitcase. Lieutenant Romayko said he'd send some officers to meet her at the bus station.

At the same time Bobbie and Carl pulled up in a taxi. They had just been released from jail. Bobbie was now more determined than ever to find out where the coins were hidden.

"Follow 'em," Bobbie ordered the cab driver. The taxi roared off after Ray's car.

It took twenty minutes for Theresa to follow Ray and Timmy to the Greyhound bus station. Once there, she got out of her car and followed them into the crowded terminal. She watched as Ray and Timmy joined a line at the bus ticket counter.

"You get on that bus," Ray warned Timmy, "you're making a big mistake."

"I'm not the one making the mistake, Dad," replied Timmy defiantly. "My bus is going to Redding. Yours is going to Folsom Prison."

"Would you stop with that!" said Ray. They stepped up to the ticket counter. "Last chance. You staying or not?"

"That's up to you," said Timmy.

Ray paused. He knew he had no choice in the matter. "One-way ticket to Redding," he said to the ticket agent as he pulled his wallet from his pocket.

Just then Bobbie and Carl reached the station, jumped out of their cab and ran into the terminal.

"There they are," said Bobbie. He was pointing to Ray and Timmy at the ticket window.

"He bought a bus ticket," said Carl. "Maybe the kid is leaving."

Bobbie knew that that could mean only one thing: Timmy told Ray where the coins were and now Ray was sending him home. Bobbie angrily started toward the ticket booth, but Carl pulled him back.

"No," said Carl. "We talk to him outside. After he puts the kid on the bus." When all was said and done, Carl liked Timmy. He couldn't bear to see the boy harmed.

They watched as Timmy took his ticket and followed Ray to the bus departure area.

"You really are a little pain, you know that?" Ray asked his son.

"Thanks for teaching me about art and how to pick up girls," said Timmy.

The bus pulled up to the loading area and opened its doors. Ray and Timmy looked at each other. Timmy was hoping that Ray would change his mind and choose him over the coins.

But Ray, thinking about his big score, couldn't bring himself to make such a choice.

"It's okay, Dad," said Timmy. "I don't need a hug."

Then Timmy abruptly turned and climbed onto the bus without looking back.

Ray watched as his son walked out of his life forever.

23.
Decision

Ray turned away from the bus and pushed past the other boarding passengers. His mind was churning. *What could I do? I need the money, right? He can't expect me to give up the chance to be somebody for once.*

From across the lobby Theresa watched Ray turn away from the departure area and head toward the pay lockers. By now Ceranski, Zinn, and another plainclothes officer had joined her. They had orders not to arrest Ray until he had the coins in his hands.

Bobbie and Carl were on the opposite side of the lobby, also waiting to pounce on their ex-partner.

Ray walked up to the lockers and pulled the key from his pocket. He stood frozen there, unable to decide what to do.

"You gotta decide," he mumbled to himself. "What's more important."

"Bus number ten-sixty-five, now leaving for

Redding," came a voice over the loudspeaker. The announcer was talking about Timmy's bus. "Last call."

Ray decided. "I'm gonna regret this," he sighed wearily. He put the key back into his pocket.

He spun around and ran toward the departure gate. He skirted around the crowds of people in the station. He was praying that he wasn't too late.

He reached the departure area just as Timmy's bus was pulling out. He ran in front of the bus and signaled for the driver to stop.

"What do you want?" asked the driver as he opened the bus doors.

"My son!" answered Ray.

Ray found Timmy sitting in the last row of the bus. They looked at each other.

"Let's get one thing straight," Ray told his son. "We're gonna have to change the living arrangements because I'm not sleeping on that couch every night."

A big smile broke across Timmy's face as he ran up the aisle. He didn't stop until he was snuggled tightly in Ray's arms.

It was the hug he had been waiting for.

Ray pulled Timmy's suitcase down from the luggage rack and led Timmy off the bus and back into the terminal.

"How 'bout if we move?" Timmy asked excitedly. "We can get a two-bedroom place."

"Oh, sure," sighed Ray. "Like I can afford that now."

They paused as they reached the row of pay lockers.

"What if I just took *some* of the coins," Ray said wistfully. "You know, five or six, just for the expenses." Ray could see Timmy's happy expression begin to drop. "Fine," he said. "So I don't buy the bakery."

Timmy smiled again. "So we save our money," he said. "You'll get it someday. C'mon, Dad. Let's get out of here."

They were just about to move on when Bobbie stepped in front of them.

"Open the locker," he snarled at them. Ray and Timmy froze. Bobbie was aiming a gun at them. "Open the locker, Ray. And give me the coins. I know they're in there."

"Aw, Bob, put that away," urged Ray. "You know you're not gonna do anything with that."

"You never take me seriously, Ray," he said gripping the gun tighter. "But you're taking me seriously now. Open the locker!"

Ray could see that Bobbie meant business. "All right, Bob," he agreed. "Okay."

Ray took the key from his pocket and opened the locker. Inside was the blue sports bag that Timmy had put there. He took it out. Bobbie smiled.

"*Freeze!*" came Ceranski's voice from behind

them. Ray and Bobbie turned. Ceranski and the other officers were instantly upon them, their guns drawn. Ray and Bobbie put their hands up.

"Ray Gleason, Bobbie Drace," said Ceranski. "You're under arrest." He grabbed the sports bag and then clamped handcuffs on Ray and Bobbie. "You have the right to remain silent. If you give up that right anything you say can and will be used against you in a court of law."

From across the lobby Carl watched and shook his head sadly. He had refused to follow Bobbie. He didn't want to hurt Timmy. Now he turned and walked out of the bus terminal.

It was all over.

24.
The Coins

"Dad, what's going on?" asked Timmy as he watched the police read Ray and Bobbie their rights.

"I think somebody made a big mistake, Tim," said Ray.

"Yeah," Bobbie said insistently. "I haven't done anything!"

Just then Ray looked up to see Theresa standing behind Timmy. He realized she was a cop, too.

"I'm sorry, Ray," was all Theresa could say. "I'm sorry."

Ray looked at her as if he were sorry, too.

Theresa nodded to Ceranski. He unzipped the sports bag and looked in eagerly.

Then his eager expression froze. He held the open bag for everyone to see. It was filled to the zipper with coins. But these coins were pennies.

And not one of them was worth more than one cent.

After returning to police headquarters, Theresa

placed Ray and Bobbie in a detention cell. Then she brought Timmy to a small bare room that was usually used to interrogate suspects.

"Okay," began Theresa. "Now, you say you put the pennies in the bag and put it in the locker."

"Uh-huh," Timmy answered innocently. "Is that against the law?"

"No," replied Theresa. "But why did you do it?"

"I won the pennies playing poker and I didn't want them stolen," was Timmy's explanation.

Theresa smiled. "You know I'm your friend, Timmy," she said gently.

"I know," smiled Timmy. "Want to come for dinner tonight?"

"Timmy, this is a very serious matter," Theresa began to explain. "Over a million dollars in coins have been stolen and I want you to tell me everything you know about the robbery."

Timmy pondered for a moment. "Do you have a boyfriend?" he asked.

"Timmy — "

"I thought we were friends," Timmy interrupted. "I'm just asking a question."

"No, I don't have a boyfriend."

"You must be pretty lonely, huh?" asked Timmy. "It was like that after my mom died. It hurt a lot and I never thought it'd go away. But now I got my dad back and I'm still going to miss her. But I think it's going to be okay. And I know whoever stole those coins is real sorry they did it and they'll never steal anything ever again."

Theresa looked at Timmy. She realized that he wasn't going to tell her anything.

"That's wonderful, Tim," she said. "But the coins are still missing. Could you 'guess' where they might be?"

Timmy shrugged. "I don't know," he said, leading her on. "They could be in a bag maybe."

"Like the bag you put your pennies in?"

"Yeah," answered Timmy. "And maybe people could walk past it and not know it's in there. Maybe the guy holding it doesn't even know."

Theresa suddenly remembered the last place she had seen such a bag. She bolted from the interrogation room and drove to the same department store where Timmy had given her the White Linen perfume. There, on the mannequin just inside the front entrance, was the blue sports bag.

She took the bag off the mannequin's shoulder, opened it, and looked inside. She smiled.

It was filled with the stolen coins.

136

25.
A New Life

Ray was released from the detention cell later that day. He was told that no charges would be filed against him because of lack of evidence. The same held true for Bobbie. The police department would return the coins to the Coin Grading Service, having found them as a result of an *anonymous tip*.

Ray waited in the lobby of the police station. After a few moments a door opened and Theresa appeared with Timmy.

"Let's go home, Dad," said Timmy.

Ray looked at Theresa. "It's like I said about cops," he reminded her. "They assume too much. Some things aren't always what they seem."

Theresa smiled. "And sometimes they are," she began, "but you just can't prove it."

They looked at each other. For a long moment Ray wished Theresa wasn't a cop and Theresa wished Ray wasn't an ex-con.

"So you coming for dinner tonight?" Timmy asked Theresa innocently.

"Maybe some other time, Tim," Ray answered for Theresa. "You see, there's this thing about cops and ex-cons. There's kind of an official waiting period between the time they arrest you and the time you can ask one out."

"You take care of him," Theresa told Ray, nodding toward Timmy.

"*I* will!" said Timmy. It was true. He wasn't going to let his father get into any kind of trouble again.

Timmy and Ray left the police station and headed down the street.

"Wait till I get you home," Ray said to Timmy. "You *knew* the cops were watching and you didn't tell me!"

" 'Cause you would've tried to outsmart them and got caught," explained Timmy. "So while no one was looking, I took the bag and switched it for the one on the mannequin. And put that one in the locker."

"Yeah," said Ray. "But you let me *open* the locker and get arrested."

Timmy smiled sheepishly. "I guess you learned a lesson, huh?" he asked.

"Yeah," agreed Ray. "*Never* have children."

"Admit it," Timmy prodded. "If it wasn't for me, you'd be rotting in stir."

"At least I'd have a bed to sleep in."

They stopped at the corner and waited for the light to change.

"So what do you want to do now, Dad?" asked Timmy.

"Well," Ray said with a laugh. "I just lost a quarter million bucks and gained a permanent house guest. How 'bout I go drown myself?"

"How 'bout we go shoot hoops and pick up girls?" suggested Timmy.

Ray nodded. "We can do that."

Ray was finally acting like a real dad. Only this time Timmy knew he wasn't just pretending. Timmy smiled.

He had gotten everything he had ever wanted.

He was eager to begin his new life with his dad.